Praise for the

AN UNEXPECTED FATHER
Second novel in the Collingwood Series

"**A poignant, evocative, and engaging read...**Engrossing and elegant, Fillis' second installment in the Collingwood Series explores relationships, endurance, desires, and means of survival. Winson and Caitlin are man and wife now, much to the dismay of the latter's father. The pain of separation from his family weighs heavy on Winson's mind, but his bond with Julian gives him strength. When a tragedy strikes, Winson becomes Julian's most trusting aid, but there are people who despise his Chinese roots, and with Tak and Dung back, his dream of having a normal life becomes a distant possibility. Fillis skillfully captures the pain of loss and the resiliency of the human spirit, and his crisp prose keeps readers turning pages fast. Winson's relationship with Julian, his bond with Kai, his apprehensions about being an immigrant and acceptance, and Caitlin's unwavering trust in him are all beautifully portrayed. This fascinating coming-of-age journey, focusing on the strength of family and friendship, forgiveness, redemption, integrity, racism, and issues of immigration, will appeal to a wide readership. Fans of historical fiction will be enthralled."

–THE PRAIRIES BOOK REVIEW ★ ★ ★ ★

A HEART TO SURVIVE
First novel in the Collingwood Series

Haunting, poignant, and compelling... Human trafficking, racial disparity, resilience, and courage mark Fillis's earnest series kicker in the historical fiction series. With the civil war in full swing and Mao Zedong's ruthless control of the nation, fourteen-year-old Tao Wen Shun, the upstanding son of an educated family, is sent aboard a sailing ship to live as the paper-son to a Chinese family in Canada. After a harrowing sea voyage, Tao finds himself in the clutches of a human trafficking gang, and escape doesn't seem like an option. The world Fillis creates, be it the disquiet of a Chinese town of Hangzhou or the searing discrimination of a Canadian city, is both complex and authentic. The warm, grounded romance toward the end comes out as a pleasant surprise. Although the novel tackles various complex themes, including human trafficking, racial discrimination, young love, and a teenager's coming of age story, Fillis's expert execution of the plot and sharp cultural observations make it a gratifying read.

–THE PRAIRIES BOOK REVIEW ★ ★ ★ ★ ★

In this sharp-edged, dark historical drama, a young Chinese boy's attempt at a normal life in Canada crumbles after he falls prey to a human trafficking ring. It's the peak of the civil war in China. With Mao Zedong's rebel forces gaining momentum, fourteen-year-old Tao Wen Shun is forced to board a ship to Canada by his family to escape the terrors of Mao's regime. But instead of a Chinese family awaiting him on the other side, he finds himself trapped in the clutches of a human trafficking ring. Fillis skillfully chronicles Wen's courageous ascent to liberation, imbuing his story with a sense of claustrophobia and hope. Wen Shun is gutsy, resourceful, and keen to help others, and his journey to freedom is inspiring as he remains standing tall in the face of the relentless difficulties life throw his way. Crisp prose, the affecting first-person narrative, and tension-filled, tight plotting keep the readers turning pages nonstop. The conclusion is left unresolved, leaving readers excited for the next installment. Paired with the atmospheric setting, the exploration of the themes of human trafficking, racial discrimination, and individual struggles makes for a thoroughly engrossing coming of age tale.

BOOK VIEW REVIEW ★ ★ ★ ★

Author's website:
GeorgeFillisNovels.com

George Fillis

AN
UNEXPECTED
FATHER

second novel in the Collingwood Series

An Unexpected Father / George Fillis

ISBN: 978-1-7359372-2-9 (Print)
ISBN: 978-1-7359372-3-6 (Ebook)

Printed in the United States of America

Publisher: Bluerock7, LLC.
Book Design by Berge Design
Cover Image by Doug Burlock Photography

For Karen with all my Love and Gratitude

And to Dr. Lew Spurlock for his friendship
and literary mentoring

Contents

Nicht Fleisch und Blut, das Herz macht uns zu Vätern and Söhnen.

Johann Friedrich von Schiller
Die Räuber, Act 1, Scene 1

It is not flesh and blood but the heart which makes us fathers and sons.

Chapter One

Collingwood, Ontario | 1959

Beneath the massive gray and white clouds billowing above Collingwood and racing to fill the sky in every direction, the leaves ignited into various shades of red and gold. Smoke swirled out of chimneys with the smell of burning logs. The temperature had fallen, and a brisk wind came off the bay as the wedding party made its way into the African Baptist Episcopal Church on Seventh Avenue.

Caitlin looked beautiful as she walked down the aisle wearing an ivory silk suit and a pill-box hat. Her long auburn hair curled below her shoulders and a contagious smile spread across her face, highlighting her bright blue eyes. My stomach was in knots, but I was the happiest man on earth.

I hoped Caitlin wasn't too disappointed that her mother didn't walk her down the aisle. Caitlin's father was still angry that his Irish daughter was marrying a man from China. He was adamant when he refused to attend the wedding. Caitlin said that her mother agreed to give her away, but her father would have none of it and told her, "If she's going to marry him, then by God, I'm not going to allow it to be a spectacle for everybody in the whole town."

When Caitlin walked down the aisle accompanied by Catherine, I was delighted. Everything good that had happened to me since coming to Collingwood came through Catherine. I shared a closeness with Catherine like the one I had in China with my grandfather, YeYe. He had shaped my perspectives on life.

Every time I looked at Caitlin, her sparkling eyes were open wide, and she looked confident and radiant. I never thought I would marry, and it was beyond my wildest imagination to wed such a wonderful woman. My stomach began to spasm, and I was on-the-brink of tears, but when Caitlin took my hand and calmed me with her eyes, joy swelled inside me, and the world seemed a different place, full of grace and light.

After the ceremony, we were surrounded by our friends. Kai was my best man, which was only fitting since he had journeyed with me from Hangzhou. Kathleen's parents and her husband, Patrick, were invited, but they chose not to attend like the Mulroney's.

The wedding party was seated at the head table, and at the table next to us was my employer, Mr. Julian LeBlanc, sitting in his wheelchair dressed in his finest suit. My good friend Jackson was seated next to him and assisted him while Virginia, his nurse, and Rhoda, his housekeeper, were on his other side. I smiled at them, and they beamed back, happy for my good fortune. They all loved Caitlin.

The Coffey sisters, who helped me recover from injuries sustained from the thugs sent by Caitlin's father, were in the back of the room, making sure the refreshments were perfect. Kai's girlfriend, Wei Lei, was busy talking with them, and I was sure she told them about the peanuts she brought, explaining how peanuts were a traditional Chinese symbol for health, good fortune, and many children.

I whispered to Caitlin, "Did you notice Jackson and Kai, each holding hands with their girlfriends? Kai's feelings for

Wei Lei have grown ever since he met her at Cott's Cleaners. They have known each other longer than we have."

She smiled and whispered back, "Ruth told me Jackson and Mildred have been talking about a wedding date, and I saw them hugging outside the church this morning."

"Jackson said he loves Mildred and wants to settle down."

Kai was grinning as he and Wei Lei approached us during the reception. "Winson and Caitlin, you motivated me to ask Wei Lei's father for permission to marry her, and he said yes."

"But what did Wei Lei say?" I asked, winking at Wei Lei.

She blushed, and Kai elbowed me as he said, "Ask her yourself."

Caitlin took hold of Wei Lei's hand and said, "I'm so happy for you both. What are your wedding plans?"

"A small wedding with family and friends."

"I hope you'll be as happy as we are," Caitlin said.

"We marry for love like you," Wei Lei responded.

Kai asked, "Will you be our witnesses?"

"I'd be delighted," Caitlin said.

"I'm not sure!" I replied.

Kai looked at me, frowned, and then broke into a wide grin. We were fourteen years old when we met on the ship to Vancouver to escape the horrors of Mao Zedong. Only to discover that we were prisoners of a trafficking ring and held in a remote British Columbia logging camp. It had been eight years since we escaped.

With laughter in my voice, I asked, "When is the wedding?"

"In three weeks, on Sunday, we didn't want to conflict with your wedding ceremony," he said.

"That's wonderful. We'll make sure to be ready for the ceremony, and we'll bring lots of peanuts. Where will you live?"

"We'll live with Wei Lei's parents until we can afford a place of our own."

All of a sudden a red knitted cap was pulled down over my head. There was laughter as I lifted it off and saw Jackson and Mildred, both with big smiles. As Mildred handed a white one to Caitlin, she said, "These toques are your wedding presents."

Jackson said, "Catherine knitted one for each of you with the national colors of Canada."

I owed a lot to Jackson. He knew the train porters, so he planned an escape for Kai and me from the logging camp by hopping a train to Collingwood. Caitlin and I hugged Jackson and Mildred, then I asked, "Should I speak to Catherine about working on two more toques?"

Mildred flashed a big smile and said, "One never knows." I was amazed at the events taking place and how all our lives were changing.

Mr. LeBlanc was sitting with Virginia and Rhoda when Caitlin and I approached them. As a quadriplegic, he required around the clock care and being his personal assistant, Caitlin and I would live in his home.

With a warmhearted smile Mr. LeBlanc said, "Well this is the beginning of a wonderful life for the two of you. I have something for you, but please don't open it until you get home this evening. Virginia, please give them my gift,"

Virginia handed an envelope to Caitlin.

"May I kiss you, Mr. LeBlanc?" Caitlin asked.

"Anytime. You're my daughter now." Then she kissed him on both cheeks.

While Caitlin continued talking with Julian and Virginia, Kathleen tapped me on the shoulder. We stepped away, and she turned her back away from the crowd. It was just the two of us as she faced me and reached for my hand. Looking down, she said, "Caitlin and I have known each other since we were infants. When she told me she was in love, I was ecstatic for her. But when I discovered that you were Chinese, I was disheartened. I am ashamed to say that I tried to talk her out of having a relationship with you."

She cocked her head and cleared her throat. I squeezed her hand, and when we made eye contact, I smiled and she continued.

"When I saw the glow on her face as she spoke about you and how you made her feel, I had second thoughts. She was heartbroken when she found out that her father instigated your beating." She stopped, looked away, and took a hard, dry swallow. "When my parents condemned Caitlin to her face for wanting to marry you, she smiled and told them the love you two have is a gift from God..."

She choked up as I pulled out a handkerchief and handed it to her. "We were raised in the church and taught to believe that all people were created equal."

Her eyes glistened with moisture, then she stepped forward, hugged me, and whispered, "I'm sorry for how I felt then, but I know better now."

"Kathleen, look at me." I held both her hands and waited until she lifted her gaze to me. Tears were running down her cheeks by now, and her lower lip was quivering. I was able only to whisper, "No apology is needed."

"Thank you, Winson. Seeing the love between you and Caitlin is something I desire in my own marriage. I am so happy for Caitlin, for both of you. I hope one day, my husband will feel the same towards you." She squeezed my hand and walked away.

Moved by what she had shared, I was hopeful that hearts would change but realized that change comes slowly. I had some time to collect my emotions before Caitlin returned. We said our goodbyes to the remaining guests, and Caitlin and I held hands as we walked the five blocks home.

Listening to the leaves blowing in the wind reminded me of applause, but the blissfulness of the day was shattered when we approached an intersection, and I saw a Chinese man dressed in black standing on a street corner watching us. He raised his arm, pointed at me, then Caitlin, then back at me. I had no doubt it was Tak.

I tried to remain calm as I looked around to see if anyone was with him. When I looked back at him, he patted his right coat pocket, where I assumed he hid a pistol.

As we continued walking, I tried to put him out of my mind when Caitlin said, "Winson, what's wrong?"

"What do you mean?"

"Don't give me that! Don't treat me like a child and lie to me, thinking that you are somehow protecting me. I'm your wife now. You can't keep anything from me if you love me. You do love me don't you?"

"Of course I do. How can you think otherwise? It's just that I recognized the Chinese man on the corner."

We were silent until Caitlin said, "Stop! Look at me and tell me who he is. Please don't keep anything from me."

When she looked at me, my heart opened as a flower to the morning sun, and I knew I couldn't keep anything from her. "Do you remember when I told you about being held prisoner in the logging camp and the men who inflicted so much horrible pain on Kai and me?"

"Was he one of them?"

"He was one of the overlords of the trafficking ring."

"You paid your debt. You shouldn't be worried."

"I paid the debt and more, but Dung, who claimed to be our sponsor, said we belonged to him, and he could hold us as long as he wanted. He kept our immigration papers and took all the money we made with Suk and Jackson from selling reconditioned leather shoes to immigrants coming off ships. We escaped with Suk's help, and then Jackson got us on a train to Collingwood." My spirits fell as I said, "I think I need to speak to Mr. LeBlanc about what to do."

"I want to be with you when you talk to him."

I had been fearful that Caitlin's father, Kierian Mulroney, might have done something to disrupt our wedding but never expected to see Tak. It was our wedding night, and I tried to put him out of my mind.

When we were alone in our bedroom, Caitlin opened the envelope from Mr. LeBlanc and read the card: 'Caitlin, this is a gift to pursue your music degree.' Enclosed was a check for $3,000. Tears rolled down her cheeks.

I took her hand and said, "A few weeks ago, Mr. LeBlanc asked about our plans. I told him your hopes of getting a university degree to teach music and the requirement to apprentice under a certified teacher. I said these were future goals since we didn't have money for your education."

As I blotted the tears trickling down her cheeks, she said, "Catherine told me at the reception that she wants to reduce her teaching load and asked if I'd consider teaching several of her beginner and intermediate students. She knew of my dream to teach and that I didn't have the money to go through certification at the Conservatory of Music in Toronto. She's the only person in the Collingwood area approved to provide a certification, and she offered her services to me as a wedding gift." We hugged and were overwhelmed.

It was the happiest day of my life. Still, I regretted that her family and friends didn't attend, and my family had no knowledge of our marriage.

The next afternoon, Caitlin and I went into Mr. LeBlanc's office. When he saw us, he beamed and said, "How are the newlyweds?"

Caitlin said, "We are in love."

He studied me, then furrowed his brow and said, "Winson, I thought you would be all smiles on the day after your wedding, but you have been preoccupied with something all morning. Tell me, what's wrong."

I looked at Caitlin, she nodded at me, then I turned to Mr. LeBlanc and said, "Do you remember when I told you about escaping from the logging camp?"

"Yes."

"I thought I saw one of my captors about a month ago on the sidewalk in front of the house. Yesterday, on our way home from the church, I saw him again. This time I am certain it is one of the bosses from camp. His name is Tak, and I'm terrified of him. He told Kai and me that they owned us, and we would never be free from them."

Mr. LeBlanc sighed deeply, "Don't jump to any conclusions."

"What do you think I should do?"

"Let me talk to my attorney, Clive Owen, and find out if anyone knows about this man and what he is doing here in Collingwood. Try not to concern yourself with anything but your beautiful bride. The good news is that he did not try to contact you in the last month, and he did not approach you yesterday. Maybe he realizes he has no claim against you."

∽

Life was exciting, but the rift between Caitlin and her father persisted. The last time Caitlin talked with him, he told her not to speak to him again unless he initiated a conversation. It stung, and she was hurt, but there was nothing she could do except honor his request. Her mother only saw her when her father was away, and I was thankful Caitlin maintained some relationship with her.

It helped when Caitlin began teaching piano to Catherine's beginner students and worked part-time as a bookkeeper at Gilpin's Hardware. She took occasional trips to the Conservatory in Toronto to pursue required courses for her music degree and was tested by Catherine.

We moved upstairs into a private suite with a sitting room, bedroom, bath, and a Guardian Ear receiver and transmitter system wired from our bedroom to Mr. LeBlanc's room. It was like our own apartment. Marriage was wonderful, and we were both happy.

One morning after breakfast, Mr. LeBlanc wanted to read about world news, so I took him into his office and clipped the newspaper on the easel. After a few minutes, Rhoda came in smiling and humming as she cleaned with a feather duster and a damp rag.

Mr. LeBlanc said, "Winson, I want to read you an article on Mao's activity in China. Turn back two pages." Reading aloud of Mao's policies and the impact on the people in China, he looked annoyed when Rhoda moved items around on his desk. He cleared his throat and when she looked at him, she stopped cleaning and stood with a hand on her hip.

"Isn't there somewhere else in this house that needs your attention?"

She pulled her mouth to the left, arched her brow, and clicked her teeth as she spun around with a "humph." We could hear her stomp her feet as she made her way to the back of the house, intent on making sure we knew her displeasure.

We both watched her leave with amazed looks, but when Mr. LeBlanc caught my eye, he became serious and said, "This article is from the viewpoint of the West. You have told me a little about leaving China and coming to Collingwood. If you're willing, I want to hear more about your experiences."

I hesitated to respond. This was an emotional subject for me, but when I remembered how open Mr. LeBlanc was about his family fleeing to Poland from the Russian Pogroms, changing names like I did, and coming with other Jewish families to Canada, I replied. "It's a painful part of my life."

He waited.

In general, I told him about my life in China, then added, "My father opposed Mao's policies and spoke out against him. My parents were afraid for me and my sister, Lijuan. They wanted to send both of us to Canada through a sponsoring program called 'Paper Family.' They were only able to send me, and it turned out to be a front for human trafficking. If my sister had been able to come, they would probably have made her a prostitute, like they did Suk's wife, Biyu."

He listened and waited until our eyes met, then said, "What I have been reading to you of Mao's policies is what your parents foresaw. They acted in your best interest, hoping you'd have a better life in Canada."

"I doubt I'll ever see them again."

"I never saw my grandparents after leaving Warsaw, but I carry them in my heart, they're a part of me."

I closed my eyes, took a deep breath, and sensed Mr. LeBlanc's intense focus. "The only reminders I have of my family are this ivory medallion I wear around my neck, which was my grandfather's, the xiao he made me, and a stuffed rat, which was a gift from my sister since I was born in the year of the rat."

"Winson, you know that I care about you?"

When I looked up at him, his eyes were full of tears.

I moved toward him, paused to see if he was receptive, then embraced him.

A meaningful emotional transfer took place, a bonding between our diverse backgrounds, cultures, and histories.

"My son, we're family. I want you and Caitlin to call me Julian from now on."

I had longed to fill the void I lost since leaving China, and destiny brought me surrogates in Julian and Catherine.

Chapter Two

1960

On the last Monday of the month, I was at the bank in the late afternoon, pulling files for Julian to review when Mr. Stromberger entered the bank. His eyebrows arched as we made eye contact for a brief moment. Over the past year, I wanted to thank him for coming to my aid when I was beaten by thugs sent by Caitlin's father every time I saw him at the bank, but he seemed stoic and unreceptive. I was determined to express my gratitude today.

As I walked up to him, he took a step back, and I noticed the tellers perk up as if I were not supposed to engage a customer, particularly this one.

I said in a low voice, "Excuse me Mr. Stromberger, but I want to thank you for your assistance when I was attacked. You saved my life!"

"Winson! Winson!" The sound of the voice was like a mallet hitting a gong. I stiffened as Taylor, the bank president, came up from behind me, took a position between us, and said in his whiny voice, "Mr. Stromberger, so good to see you. May I be of help?"

Taylor extended his hand to him, then turned to me and said firmly, "Winson, don't you have something to do back in the file room?"

Stromberger looked at me, then at Taylor, and said, "Good to see you, Mr. Taylor. I'm just making a deposit." He glanced at me, paused, then looked back at Taylor. "Please give me a minute with this young man."

Taylor replied, "Certainly, just let me know if I can be of assistance." He turned his back to Stromberger and gave me a contemptuous scowl as he walked away.

Stromberger spoke in a voice that was just above a whisper, "Your clothes were saturated with blood, and you drifted in and out of consciousness. Who was the man that helped me carry you?"

"His name is Jackson, and he's like a brother to me."

"I couldn't have lifted you without his help. You're a big guy even though you're thin. Those six men looked like they were trying to kill you. If you don't mind my asking, what was the fight over?"

"My seeing an Irish girl."

"I detest discrimination." His comment surprised me, and I caught him looking in the direction of Taylor's office.

"I would like to do something for you to repay your kindness."

"You owe me nothing. It was the right thing to do, and if it wasn't me, there would've been another person to help. My first instinct was that you needed to go to the hospital, but your friend insisted we take you to the church. Apparently, they took good care of you, and I'm glad there were no permanent injuries."

He looked around, and the tellers were watching us. "If you'll excuse me, I'll make my deposit and return to my business." He hesitated, then cleared his throat and asked, "After work, would you like to come to the Collingwood Inn, and we can talk where it'll be more private."

"I'd appreciate the opportunity."

After he left, Taylor came up to me and said in a haughty tone, loud enough for the staff to hear, "Don't you ever approach a customer again without getting express permission from me. Is that clear, Boy?"

"Yes, Sir."

"Stick to getting files for the old man. I could say one thing to LeBlanc, and you'd be fired. Don't ever forget that!" He glared at me and said in an icy voice that was meant to threaten, "I'm watching you and know everything about you. Now get back to your work."

It felt like all the bank employees were watching, and when he turned and looked around, the staff all dropped their heads and went back to their work.

As I left the bank and walked toward the Collingwood Inn, I saw the man who had been stalking me for months. Jackson had told me his name was Jay, and when I passed him he began walking in my direction. Before entering the Inn, I turned and stared at him as he leaned against a light post and lit a cigarette then walked up to face him and said, "Tell Taylor I know you're following me. I'm sure Mr. LeBlanc would like to know how his money is being spent." With a snarl, he shrugged and took a puff. As I walked away I no longer thought Caitlin's father hired him but knew it must be Taylor.

Stromberger greeted me with a smile and said, "Would you like a tour of the premises before we have refreshments on the patio?"

"I would enjoy a tour."

The Inn was in pristine condition, and the gardens were filled with a colorful mix of beautiful flowers and shrubs.

"When my wife and I were in France, we visited Monet's country home and gardens in Giverny. Impressed by what we saw, we remodeled the Inn after it. The wall colors and the dark, rough wood beams overhead are similar to his home, and the pictures are copies of Monet's paintings. The rooms are all decorated with antique country French furniture."

He led me to an outside porch shaded by a ring of tall weeping willows, where we sat at a wicker table with cushioned armchairs and fresh flowers in a crystal vase. It was a comfortable and beautiful setting as we looked out on a garden of flowers in full bloom.

"I have ordered tea and chocolate croissants. I hope that's acceptable?"

"Yes, Sir, and thank you for having me."

"My pleasure. Here comes Melissa with our treats." She placed the tray on the table and proceeded to serve Stromberger.

"Melissa, you know to serve our guests first."

She turned toward me, pressed her eyelids together, then stared daggers as she placed the tea and chocolate croissant before me. I could smell the warm croissant, but that was the only warmth between her and me.

"Thank you, Miss Pittard. I'm pleased to see you again," I said.

She tipped her head upward and turned toward Stromberger, who frowned as she departed.

"I apologize for the service. It's most unlike Melissa, but it's obvious that you know her."

"We share a mutual interest in music and have taken lessons from the same teacher."

"Oh yes, she takes piano lessons from Catherine DeVeaux."

When Catherine had introduced me to Miss Pittard several years ago, she refused to acknowledge me, even after Catherine confronted her, so I decided to change topics. "Did you say you were from Europe?"

"I was born and raised in Vienna, Austria. During the war, my father was arrested by the Gestapo when he spoke out against Hitler. The Nazis shot him when he was on his way to a concentration camp because he walked with a limp and had trouble keeping up."

"Oh my, what a tragedy, I'm so sorry. My father spoke out against Mao in China and faced arrest, but I don't know what happened to him since I left before his trial. I don't think we ever get over such incidents, we just learn to compensate."

He gave me a nod of approval, then leaned forward and poured more tea. We spent about an hour sharing our stories with each other. At the bank, he was resigned and seemed out of reach, but now was comfortable one on one, perhaps due to his being in familiar surroundings. Nevertheless, I felt a rapport with him.

"Why did you come to Canada?" I asked.

"I was ready for a change. I trained as a chef in Switzerland and France and found a job in a large hotel kitchen as a sous chef, after traveling by steamship to Halifax and train to Toronto. I was promoted to chef after a few years and wanted more out of life. In the mornings, I went to school, worked at night, and eventually was promoted into management. Then I got lucky!

"In the hotel lobby, I met a beautiful young lady. We were drawn to each other immediately and married six months later. Her father was Jewish, and the Nazis killed him, but she escaped to England with her mother and siblings. A Jewish family brought them to Canada, and they lived as one big family. Despite what they endured during the war, they were empathetic and embraced me as a German-speaking Austrian, and they are my extended family. Exposure to them broadened my vision, taught me about the Jewish culture and religion, and introduced me to French and Canadian cultures.."

That was so different from the circumstances in which I came to Canada.

"Tell me about your Irish girl."

"I was introduced to Caitlin through Miss DeVeaux."

"From the ring on your finger, did you marry her?"

I started fidgeting with the ring and said, "I did, and never dreamed we could be so happy together."

"What about her family?"

"We don't have a relationship. She occasionally sees her mother, but her father has nothing to do with us."

"Maybe one day that will change."

I shifted uncomfortably in my chair. "Maybe," I said without much conviction. "Why did you buy the Inn?"

"My wife and I both worked long hours in Toronto, seven days a week. After a few years of marriage, I wanted to prove myself. The hotel business is a young man's endeavor. We were ready to invest in a small hotel of our own and found this rundown Inn in Collingwood about seven years ago at a price we could afford. We purchased it, worked hard to improve the property, and in time grew the business and continued making improvements. Edith enjoyed planting tulips in the fall before the first frost and then seeing them bloom in the spring."

"I haven't seen Mrs. Stromberger with you at the bank."

He looked off into the distance, adjusted how he was sitting, then choked up as he said, "Edith suffered from constant back pain that wouldn't go away. We thought it was from working so hard redoing the hotel and landscaping, but the pain intensified, and when she couldn't continue her normal activities, we went to see a specialist in Toronto, who diagnosed her with bone cancer in her spine."

He looked away, and his face saddened. "Edith was my life, and her death zapped my energy."

"I am sorry. Life must be difficult without her. I can't imagine my life without Caitlin."

We were silent until he changed the subject. "Immigrants must work harder to prove themselves. I was fortunate because the people I met in Canada were good and looked past my shortcomings."

I was surprised when he took hold of my arm and said, "You must force yourself to assimilate." I thought of Mother telling me the same thing and not to look back but only ahead.

"How did you get to Canada?" he asked.

He was so different from my first impression, and his interest caused me to open up. I told him the story of my life, and then he asked, "Do you have contact with your family in China?"

"No. No, not since the day I left, I have never received a letter. I've written them many times but without reply. I have no idea where they are or if they're still alive."

"Our paths have crossed for a reason. I'm fifty years old, and when I look back on my life, leaving Europe was the best thing I've ever done. There has been an entrenched class system there for centuries. If your family didn't have anything when you were born, you could never do much with your life. Your parents most likely had a vision in mind for you, but there were unknown circumstances beyond their knowledge." He raised his eyebrows, and his eyes brightened as he said, "The immigrants who arrive first make the rules. The Chinese syndicate is an example. If you can overcome them, you may be able to help others who become similarly entangled."

"Thank you, I will think about what I can do."

I thanked him for the visit and, on my way out, bid a pleasant goodbye to Miss Pittard.

Jay was still on the corner, smoking a cigarette. I hadn't told Caitlin or Julian of his presence, but his shadowing me was annoying. I looked directly at him and said, "I'm on my way home, you know the way. You might not keep this job much longer."

I stood on the porch when I got home, and Jay just stood across the street. I ignored him and watched the sunset igniting the sky into shades of fiery red and orange, and in the distance, dark clouds rolled over the horizon, riding the summer winds.

That night, as I looked in the mirror, thinking of Stromberger, I had judged him by my first impression without understanding his background. I determined not to prejudge and realized that everyone is fighting their own hard and mostly unseen battles. I needed to look for and consider my own biases.

Chapter Three

It was almost dark when Kai rushed in the back door of Julian's house a few weeks later. His face was red and flushed, and he stammered so severely I couldn't understand him.

"Slow down, Kai. What's wrong?"

He slurred words, and all I understood was Tak. I forced him to sit and gave him a glass of water.

"What about Tak."

"H..h..he's here!"

"You saw him?"

He nodded.

"Did he see you?"

"He came out of Drott's, w..w..we passed each other on the street. I didn't think he recognized me, but then h..h..he laughed and called me cauliflower."

Kai rubbed on his ear, grimaced, and raised his eyebrows. "H..h..he asked about you. I didn't say anything. He said he knew where you lived."

"I saw him on my wedding day. That was several months ago, but nothing has come of it. What do you think he is doing in Collingwood?"

"He is selling wood. Ah..ah..ah…"

"Slow down, sip more water."

"H..h..he..." Beads of sweat began to bubble on Kai's skin.

"Did he threaten you?"

He nodded.

"What did he say?"

"Dung has been looking for us."

"We paid our debts."

"He said it was important to meet. He's at the Harbor Park Hotel for two days and he gave me this. Tell me what it says?"

Kai handed me a newspaper, and I read it to myself first.

"The front-page article is titled *Kin for Hire*. It describes an investigation into what is believed to be widespread wholesale smuggling of Chinese immigrants into Canada. It's suspected there's a syndicate of smugglers providing fake Canadian relatives for potential Chinese immigrants. The Hong Kong Police are working with the Royal Canadian Mounted Police to crack down on illegal immigration from Vancouver to Montreal, and the RCMP is screening twenty thousand names."

"The p..p..police should be investigating Tak and Dung's operations."

"The police should arrest them."

"I don't want to see him again."

"Why would he be giving you this article?"

"Maybe we're the illegal immigrants, and they're going to turn us in." Kai chuckled, but there was more to what he said than he realized.

"Dung and Tak paid off the Chilliwack Policeman we ran into, and Suk said they bribed officials so they could harvest logs without permits. We know they run prostitution and protection operations."

"I'm s..s..scared."

"They work both sides of the law and may threaten to turn us over to the authorities. When I saw Tak before, I spoke to Julian, and he contacted his attorney, but Mr. Owen could not find anything about him because I didn't know his full name. I'll talk with Julian again."

Kai fidgeted, and his eyes were large and darting.

I put my hand on his shoulders and said, "Do you want a cigarette?"

"You don't smoke anymore!"

He was right. I didn't have a cigarette to offer him.

∽

The next morning, I met with Julian, updated him about Tak, read him the newspaper article, and then we phoned Clive. After hanging up, Julian said, "Clive said you need to find out what Tak wants, and the only way to do that is to meet him. Take Kai and be sure to meet in a public area with plenty of people around. When we find out what his angle is, then we can discuss strategy. Clive said if you can get his full name, it would be helpful."

Kai wouldn't want to go, but if Tak planned an ambush, I needed him. Kai came to Julian's house after work, and I explained what Clive suggested. "We should see Tak before it gets dark. There are two of us, and we should be safe if we meet him at the hotel."

As I suspected, Kai shrugged, shuffled his feet, then said, "I don't want to go."

"You don't have a choice. We're going together."

I dressed in jeans and a t-shirt, so Tak wouldn't have any idea about my employment. Neither of us spoke on the way to the hotel. Tak represented part of our past that we wanted to bury. We entered the hotel and saw him seated at the bar in a black suit and silk shirt. When he saw us, he stood and walked toward us, carrying his beer in his left hand and patting the bulge in his jacket pocket with his right hand. He looked us up and down.

"Well, if it isn't the boys who thought they were man enough to escape from camp. Let's go to my room so we can talk privately."

"Let's go out to the porch, it will be private enough," I said.

He glared at me and motioned us to lead the way. I was nervous about having him behind me and my muscles tensed until we sat at a table at the far end of the porch. There were people at other tables with food and drinks, engaged in casual conversations. They stared at us as if we were out of place.

Tak frowned at us as a bar waitress came to the table and asked Tak, "Would you like another beer?"

"Doll, I'll have another beer and anything else you want to offer."

She gave him a patronizing look, then turned to us and asked, "Would you like a drink?"

"Doll, they don't want anything." He reached into his pants pocket, pulled out a wad of bills, peeled off several, handed them to her, and held her hand tight as he told her to keep the change.

After she left the table, Tak looked deliberately at each of us, then said, "We're working with the RCMP and the Hong Kong Police. We're providing names and documents of those we know entered the country illegally."

"Your operation is illegal. Why aren't the RCMP arresting and deporting you and Dung?" I asked.

He pushed back his chair, leaned forward, and gritted his teeth. "You're rude and arrogant and should know your place!"

When he reached toward his coat, Kai and I jumped up, and my chair fell backward.

Tak looked at us like he did when he cut Kai with a knife, then glanced around at the other people on the porch who looked to see what caused the commotion.

"Let's all sit down, relax," he said in Mandarin, as he waved us toward our seats. I was tingling inside and mindful of his every move. I kept my eyes on him as I set my chair upright.

The tension broke as the waitress came with another beer. She looked at me and departed quickly.

Tak took a swallow, then looked at me with lifeless eyes. "You know we have friends in high places who we have to keep satisfied. We need $1,000 from each of you if you want us to remain quiet on how the two of you entered Canada."

Kai shuddered.

"We have no money," I said.

He took a drag on his cigarette, stared at me hard, and said, "If you don't want to be deported, you better borrow it from a relative or friend, or whoever you know in that fancy house."

I felt all the blood leave my face and neck, and when I looked back at him, he was glaring at Kai.

Kai blurted, "I c..c..can't go back,"

"Why not?" Tak said harshly, in Mandarin.

I tried kicking Kai's leg under the table to keep quiet, but it was too late.

"I'm m..m..married."

He should've never mentioned anything personal. I felt flushed, but I needed to wait out my fear.

Tak seized on the information. "Is she Chinese? Or did you find a white girl like your friend here?"

Kai realized his mistake and lowered his head.

"If she's Chinese, maybe her family came here illegally, too," Tak said.

The color had left Kai's face.

"We are searching this area for laundry and restaurant workers who owe us. What's her family name?"

I tried misdirection. "We don't know how to raise the money. We barely make enough to survive."

"Sell more of your shoes, or we can make arrangements for you to work it off." He didn't look at me but continued to stare at Kai.

"We need time to see what we can raise, when will you return?" I asked.

"I return to Collingwood on the 27th of next month for business. Meet me here. By the way, what names do you boys go by these days?"

I could not ask for his name if I didn't' want to give him mine, and I felt he read my mind when he glared at me and said, "We'll find you wherever you go. Just like we found your friend from camp."

Who was he referring to? Did he mean Jackson? But Jackson had not said anything about Tak. My heart raced when I thought he insinuated Suk and Biyu.

He broke my thoughts when he banged his beer bottle on the table and said, "Meet me here on the 27th and bring your money!" He took another swig of his beer, wiped his mouth with the back of his hand, and pulled cigarettes out of his coat pocket. "I'll let Dung know I found both of you. You still owe us interest and the rest of the money you earned from that shoe business."

I clenched my teeth and gripped my fists, wanting to punch him in his face. His assertion was revolting, but I needed to maintain my composure, so I nodded at Kai, and we left without saying another word.

On the way home, Kai kept repeating, "I shouldn't have said I was m..m..married."

He put Wei Lei's family at risk, but I needed to defuse his anxiety.

"Don't say anything to Wei Lei and her family yet. Let me talk to Julian and Clive."

"I want to get away from him, even if it means leaving Collingwood."

We were both shaken. Would we ever get away from Tak and Dung? I still didn't know their full names for Clive to investigate, but maybe Clive could get Tak's name from the hotel register, otherwise, there was no useful information from this meeting except that they were now doing business in Collingwood.

When I told Jackson about meeting Tak and his threats, Jackson said he wasn't afraid of Tak.

I explained the conversation to Julian the next morning after breakfast, and he looked out the window and said nothing, five minutes was like five hours.

"It's time you became a legal Canadian citizen."

I didn't know what he meant.

"I will have Clive complete your papers and personally expedite your application's approval."

When I realized he was going to sponsor me, I was stunned. What he was suggesting was overwhelming, but then I thought, what about Kai? I couldn't let Kai go back to China or return to the work camp. I couldn't ask Julian to do this for me and not have an alternative for Kai and Wei Lei. I had a dilemma.

I was deep in thought when I heard, "Winson. Winson."

"Yes, Sir."

"You haven't responded."

"Excuse me, I didn't realize how much time had elapsed. I'm just overwhelmed."

"Ask Virginia to come in. I need to see her."

"What can I do for you?"

"I need Virginia."

After getting Virginia, I walked into the kitchen, sat at the table, and stared at nothing. I was at the end of myself. Did I react improperly by not responding to Julian?

I was still lost in thought when Virginia came into the kitchen. "Julian needs you, eh."

As Virginia and I walked into his office, I said, "Yes, Sir."

"I want us to talk. Sit down."

He intently looked at me. "Knowing you, you're more concerned with our friend Kai than yourself. Virginia, tell him what you have offered."

"I would like to sponsor Kai as a Canadian citizen. Clive will prepare and submit all the required documents along with yours."

I couldn't believe what was taking place.

Chapter Four

I was in the bank's file room on the 27th of the following month collecting files for Julian to review. As I exited the room, a Chinese man in a dark grey pinstripe suit caught my attention as he approached the tellers. I hid behind a doorway, battling the urge to run.

How did Tak know I was at the bank? He said he'd return to Collingwood today, and I was supposed to meet him at the hotel. If he saw Kai or me, he'd demand $1,000 from each of us, and I didn't know what to expect when we told him we didn't have the money.

The teller helping Tak walked over to Colin Cheek, the Head Cashier. When Mr. Cheek saw Tak, he went around the teller area, shook hands with him, patted him on the back like an old friend, then offered Tak a cigar and grinned as he led Tak into Taylor's office. I didn't want to be confronted by Tak, especially in Taylor and Cheek's presence, so I left the bank in a hurry.

Julian was resting when I arrived home, and I was apprehensive as I waited in our bedroom until Caitlin arrived. I was always happy to see her, but particularly so today, as I hugged her and kissed both of her cheeks. I did not want to let go, and she detected my anxiety as she said, "What's wrong?"

"We need to talk," I said as I ended our embrace. "I saw Tak at the bank today. He greeted Mr. Cheek like an old friend, then went in to see Mr. Taylor. I left the bank in a panic before they could see me. He probably knows where I work and asked Taylor about me."

She took my hand and said, "That may or may not be so. Tak and Dung obviously have a business in Collingwood, and they need a bank account."

"They operate in cash and pay no taxes."

"Maybe you should check to see if they have opened an account. Regardless, you need to tell Julian."

"What if Tak sees me at the bank?"

"Go either before or after the bank is open to the public."

I couldn't sleep that night as I had flashbacks of the camp and being jailed. Tak saw me entering Mr. LeBlanc's house and again on the street with Caitlin on our wedding day. Where else had he seen me? Taylor and Cheek were very friendly with him, and they didn't like me.

∾

The next morning I told Julian about seeing Tak at the bank and how Taylor and Cheek had greeted him. "I wonder if Taylor and Cheek know Tak is a thug," Julian said.

"I want to see if Tak opened an account?" I replied.

"If he did, we can discover his name, but then I want the account closed. They could be trouble for the bank," Julian said.

Late that afternoon, after the bank lobby was closed to customers and Taylor and Cheek were occupied, I looked up the accounts opened in the last few months for evidence of Tak or Dung. A new account was opened for *Imperial Lumber Company* with an address in Vancouver, British Columbia, and the signature on the account read Tao-ching, which I thought must be for Tak. I remembered when I met with Zhang, the agent in Hangzhou, it was at Imperial Groceries & General Merchandise. Was Imperial a coincidence?

When I returned to the house, I told Julian, "I found a new account for Imperial Lumber Company and the signatory was Tao-ching, which must be Tak's Chinese name. Maybe Imperial is selling lumber for cabinets and caskets to Drott's."

"Let's call Clive and have him investigate Tao-ching and Imperial Lumber. Also, stop by Drott's tomorrow and see what information you can discover."

∽

Mr. Drott was dressed in his usual baggy pants with suspenders when I walked into his shop early the next morning. I wore one of Julian's suits, and he didn't recognize me from when I worked for him years ago.

I was startled when he greeted me and said, "You must be working with Mr. Tak. Let me get him, eh."

My mind filled with visions of blood splattering Tak's dark green shirt and falling on the floor as he cut into Kai's ear. This brute would do anything to anyone. Since meeting him at the hotel, I woke up in the night with sweats and saw his face in the shadows throughout the day. I decided to leave as soon as Mr. Drott left the room, but as I moved toward the door, Tak came around the corner. He looked as shocked as I was, and it took him a moment to harden his expression, as he said in Mandarin, "My little lost rat. What are you doing dressed up like that?"

When I didn't answer, he leaned toward me, and saliva filled his mouth. "Where are you working?"

Mr. Drott said, "I don't understand what the two of you are saying and have work to do if you don't need me."

I replied in English, "Sir, I have no business with this man. I'm leaving."

Tak continued speaking in Mandarin as I turned to walk out, "We will track you down. We're doing business in Collingwood, and I'll have my eyes out looking for you and your stupid friend. Expect me!"

Chapter Five

Simco Shipyard | *1962* | *Montebello*

L aunch day in Collingwood was a spectacular event. All week, television, newspapers, and radio crews had been in town, joined by excited locals and tourists vying to find seats to see the *Montebello's* launch. Collingwood's harbor was small and not very deep which required ships built at Simco Shipyard to be launched sideways. At most shipyards, new ships were end launched or built in dry docks that were flooded with water.

Schools were out, and even though the launch was scheduled for noon, families came hours early to line along the causeway to the silos or sit on building rooftops near the ship.

I told Caitlin during breakfast that I wanted to see the launch. She said, "Mildred told me that Jackson was working overtime and told her that Montebello was a beast of a ship to build, and the staff had been reduced in prior weeks, which meant extra work and tension for those who remained."

"The last time I saw Kai, he was struggling with the overtime requirements in the yard. I know each side launch is unique, but this is one I want to see firsthand. Do you want to go with me?"

"I have lessons throughout the day and have seen too many launches with my dad. Once I was on the tower with him as he gave the signal for the men to cut the lines holding the ship. That's all that was talked about at home for weeks."

When I was going through morning activities with Julian, I asked him, "Would you like to watch *Montebello's* launch today? You know she's the longest and heaviest ship ever built in Collingwood."

"I have seen enough launches in my day. A side launch is a fascinating engineering event. You're young and should watch as a spectator. Why don't you see if either Virginia or Rhoda would like to go with you?"

"I should return by one o'clock."

"Don't get too close and get wet from the backwashes," he chuckled.

I asked Virginia first and then Rhoda if they wanted to join me, but both declined. It was around 10:15 a.m. when I arrived at the harbor. Standing on a street corner across from the yard, I became part of a mass of people crowding in to witness the historic event.

I felt dwarfed by the Montebello's size. Seeing the workers driving wedges in the blocking under the ship, something seemed askew, but I couldn't put my finger on anything. I didn't know where Jackson, Kai, and Joseph were positioned, but it was somewhere under the ship. Kai and Jackson told me they'd be knocking out the dogs, the original keel blocks beneath the ship, which were no longer needed so that the ship would be positioned to slide down the launchways. Once the dogs were out, the ship was held in place by steel beams and wooden blocks, attached to wire and rope lines. Men with axes waited for a signal to cut the ropes to launch the ship.

As clouds cascaded over the mountains and blotted out the sun, I decided to get a closer look. There was a circus-like buzz of anticipation as I moved through throngs of people. I was so focused on the activity surrounding the ship that I unconsciously followed the street to the front gate of the yard and came face to face with two guards. One short and overweight, the other tall, thin, and freckle-faced, both dressed in monochromatic navy-blue uniforms with brimmed hats, both of whom undoubtedly had strict orders to only allow staff and dignitaries through the gate. The short guard held a clipboard and the other, a truncheon. I was wearing casual work clothes like I had worn when I worked in the yard.

The heavy guard with the truncheon barked, "Stop, go no further."

My eyes had been on *Montebello*, and I was startled. The thin guard with the clipboard said, "He's one of the chinks that works on the dogs. You're late, clock in, and get your ass under the ship."

The first guard's face hardened as he said, "Who do you work under?"

Surprised by the question, I blurted, "Mulroney."

Then the thin one ran his finger down a list on his clipboard, flipped a page, looked up at me, sighed, and said, "They all look alike." He waved me through.

I was startled to see so many men with sledgehammers pounding on the wedges. They were on both sides of the ship, and the sound of hammers striking wood was all I could hear. I tried to make myself invisible by walking close to the buildings, and chills went up my spine when I saw Sullivan and one of his cohorts with sledgehammers perched on their shoulders, walking straight toward me. I had made a mistake coming into their haunts. Sullivan's face hardened when he saw me but before he could speak, a loud groan emanated from the ship, and they both spun around and ran toward the gate. Even though the breeze was cool, sweat poured over my face from seeing Sullivan.

I walked toward the launch basin and glanced at the tower where Mulroney stood to signal the men to swing their axes and cut the ropes to start the launch. He was watching the men pounding sledgehammers below him. I stopped at the edge of the dock and looked across the basin. The launch basin was only about thirty feet wider than the ship itself, which seemed too narrow and shallow for a ship as large as Montebello. This launch would be complicated because if she launched too quickly or at the wrong angle, she could hit the bottom of the harbor or the basin wall, causing severe damage and threatening workers.

The infrastructure under the ship had thousands of board feet of lumber, tons of wax and grease was on the launchways and butter boards, and the cacophony of sounds was deafening from the men swinging their eight-pound sledgehammers. When the launch master gave the signal, the men with axes would cut the ropes simultaneously, and the ship would slide evenly into the launch basin. Along the dock adjacent to the ship were drag boxes, weighing several tons each, which were pulled along trenches by chains tied to the ship to keep her from going too far, too fast, and hitting the sea wall on the other side of the basin.

I turned and looked back at where I had walked from, and crowds were everywhere waiting to witness this seven-story mass of steel make its way into the waters of Georgian Bay.

I had been looking under the vessel for Jackson, Kai, or Joseph when I heard another loud groaning sound and saw an unexpected cracking and shattering of timbers and whipping of chains as the hull started to move. I jumped and moved away from the ship as she skidded down some seventy-five feet, disgorging water everywhere.

The ground shook, and my body vibrated. I felt frozen in place while screams accompanied the whistle blasts and breaking of timbers as the ship slid into the water. The men under the ship were caught in a vise between the ship and the drag chains on one side and the launch basin and sea wall on the other.

The ship's shadow covered me as she pivoted, my heart leapt, and sweat streamed down my face as men screamed and ran. I saw men fall into the water and attempt to swim away from the monstrous steel structure's movement, but there was nowhere for them to escape. Timbers exploded and hurled high into the air. The noise was deafening, and I was in shock watching this catastrophe unfold. It felt unreal, and there was no preparation or drill that anyone could have planned for this disaster. Without warning and with only seconds to run for safety, many men didn't have a chance, and bodies were either crushed or swept into the water.

I turned away, bent, and vomited. I tried to collect myself but still couldn't believe the tragic scene playing out before my eyes. I wanted to help, so I turned back toward the ship as a high wall of water swept across the basin and knocked me to the ground. It was the backwash created by the giant hull plunging into the bay. As I slowly stood and wiped the water from my eyes and nose, I felt fortunate to be out from under the launch superstructure.

Many workers under the ship couldn't escape as *Montebello* swayed back and forth on a tilt until she finally stabilized. Whistles, horns, and sirens blared as I heard emergency vehicles coming to the dock.

Eerily, the spectators were cheering, thinking the launch was successful, just early. But the yard was in chaos. Giving no thought to my safety, I had to find Kai, Jackson, and Joseph, so I pushed my way through the shipyard workers, who looked like zombies running away from the scene with glazed eyes and terrified looks on their faces. A mass of broken boards, launchways, and metal debris littered the launch site, and as I maneuvered my way around, the drag chains were still swinging back and forth.

I frantically looked at each person I came across to find my friends. Firemen and paramedics were combing the area to help the wounded as I pushed my way to a pile of sandbags and recognized Kai lying face down. When I yelled his name, and he didn't respond, I grabbed him by the shoulders and turned him over. His eyes were wide open, but he looked stunned, so I lifted him to a sitting position, and all he did was stare at the lake in a daze.

I sat next to him and tried to shake a response out of him. Had I lost my brother? I shouted, "Kai, are you all right?"

He didn't answer, so I shook him.

"Look at me Kai. Talk to me. What happened? " I could feel the bile coming up from my stomach.

When I began retching, Kai muttered, "I w..w..was under the s..s..ship, she started slipping. I was knocking out the dogs, but s..s..she started to go. I got out b..b..because the back end went first. I tried to run out between those heavy chains but had to go over the s..s..sand piles. The sand broke under my feet, and I fell. Someone stepped on my back coming from behind and drove my face into the sand. Another fellow pulled me up, and we rolled down the other side of the pile. Then a chain came and split the pile in two, right where I'd been lying. When I saw that, I fell on my face where you found me."

Ten feet from us, I saw one of the chains as thick as my arm, and only a winch could pull it.

"Are you hurt?"

"I'm okay, b..b..but Jackson…"

"Did you see Jackson?"

He shook his head.

"Will you be all right if I search for him?"

"H..h..he was at the stern."

The ship was still groaning as I stepped away from Kai, and the backwash continued to splash from the launch basin.

The water was red with blood, and rescue workers were trying to get men out of the water amidst floating body parts. Seeing a dark-skinned body floating face down, I plunged into the water, turned the man over, and when I saw it was Jackson, I choked and didn't think I could continue swimming. My body turned cold, the breath went out of me, and my heart felt like it stopped. I screamed for help, and a fireman jumped into the water and helped me get Jackson on the dock.

Jackson had been trapped under the ship, and had no escape. When *Montebello* went, he must've been knocked in the water and crushed with seven stories of metal on top of him.

As we carried him to the area designated for bodies I took deep breaths, trying to hold back sobs and struggling to recover my emotions because I still needed to find Joseph. I returned to Kai, and he shook his head when he saw the tears on my face. I hung my head and moaned, "Jackson."

I took a moment to compose myself, placed my hands on Kai's shoulders, and asked, "Will you be okay if I search for Joseph?"

He just nodded.

I hugged him and whispered, "If I don't come back soon, go home to Wei Lei when you have the strength, I'm sure she's worried. I'll check on you later." He swallowed hard and didn't respond.

I searched everywhere, calling Joseph's name, asking anyone I met if they had seen or heard about Joseph LeBlanc.

There were scuba divers from a docked U.S. frigate searching for bodies. I helped one diver get out of the water and onto the dock. He pulled off his goggles and fell backward, gasping.

"It's too murky in the water to see anything. A hard hat floated by me, I put my hand out, and when I turned it over, there was a head inside. I did everything I could to not throw up because if I vomited in my mask, I'd drown."

I spoke to a policeman who said the injured were moved to a triage area near the second gate, and the dead were transferred to a temporary morgue. I knew where that was because that's where I had taken Jackson. When I arrived at triage, I asked a nurse with bloodstains on her white uniform, "Have you seen Joseph LeBlanc?"

Her eyes were unfocused as she said with a trembling voice, "There are too many wounded to know them by name. They continue to come. Look around, but stay out of the way."

When I didn't find him, I went back and found her wrapping a tourniquet around a worker's leg. I said, "I didn't find him."

She answered, without turning her head, "There's a man in a white uniform holding a clipboard at the far end of the triage area. Ask him."

When I located him, he ignored me until I yelled twice, "Sir, I'm looking for Joseph LeBlanc?"

"LeBlanc, LeBlanc," he repeated as he checked papers on his clipboard. He didn't look up at me but continued to stare at his documents when he said, "Joseph's body was pulled out of the water and removed."

"I work for Joseph's father."

"Mr. LeBlanc, who owns Merchants Bank and Trust?"

"Yes, Sir."

"The Mayor asked for a list of the dead. I have a notation here that the Mayor will convey the news to Mr. LeBlanc."

I felt numb and knew Julian would be crushed by the news, so before the Mayor arrived, I hurried to be with him. The Mayor knew Julian since he first opened the bank, but I wanted to give him the news.

It had been six hours since I left for the shipyard, and when Julian saw me enter the house covered in filth and blood, he gasped and began to choke.

"Virginia, come quick!" I cried. Then I held Julian and said, "I'm so sorry, Sir, but Joseph didn't make it."

When she came into the room and saw Julian's face quaking, she whispered, "Go clean up. I'll give Julian some meds to calm him."

I showered quickly, and when I came back into Julian's room, I sat on his bed, gently put my arms around him, and rocked him back and forth. His eyes were puffy and bloodshot, and he stared into space saying, "There are rules for this life, and when your only child dies before you, you are nothing anymore." He sighed deeply and said, "Now he's with Ruthie."

He started weeping and moaned, "I'm full of regrets," then he convulsed. Virginia sat next to him, stroking his head, and

I held him as he sobbed until the sedatives took effect. By the time the Mayor arrived, Julian had recovered his composure, and we had changed his clothes and positioned him in his chair. I called Wei Lei to check on Kai while the Mayor offered his condolences. When we put Julian back in bed, Virginia gave him additional medication, and I spent the night in a chair next to him.

∽

After breakfast the next day, Julian said, "Take me to the office, get a pen and pad, and I will give you instructions." When I got him situated, he said, "I want you to contact Ari Green. He owns Christie's Boutique on Oak Street and is a Rabbi. He'll conduct the funeral and arrange for a traditional Jewish burial for Joseph. I only want Virginia, Rhoda, Caitlin, and you to attend."

I knew Ari as a customer at the bank but didn't realize he was a Rabbi.

Julian continued, "I want you to inspect my burial plots in the Jewish section of the cemetery. Take Rhoda with you, she knows where they are. When Ruthie died, Joseph buried her in the general cemetery without a service. When I got home from the hospital, I purchased seven plots in the Jewish cemetery, then had Ruthie moved, and Rabbi Green performed a Jewish ceremony. The other places next to her were for me, Joseph, his wife if he ever married, and their children. I haven't been there since then, and I want you to make sure the plots and area are properly prepared for Joseph's burial."

I noticed his lips were sticky. "Can I give you water to drink?"

"My mouth is dry."

"I'll get water?"

"I'd prefer Scotch." A pause followed, then he added, "Bring me both."

I could see the pain in his eyes, not only physical but emotional. After helping him sip water and Scotch on the rocks, I applied petroleum jelly to his inner lip, where he'd chewed on it, and the expression on his face softened.

∽

The next day was overcast, which contributed to the somberness of the service. Virginia gave Julian extra pain killers, and over the next few days, he wanted more medication, and his agitations only stopped while he was sleeping. He grimaced when he was awake and didn't want to speak.

Caitlin and I went to see Mildred the day after Joseph's service. She was at the church sitting around a table with the Coffey sisters and seeing us, she rose and gave each of us a long hug. She choked up and had difficulty speaking when I apologized for not being the one to tell her about Jackson's death.

Caitlin asked, "What can we do to help you?"

After a few minutes, she said, "Pastor Jones is arranging the funeral for Saturday. Jackson loved Catherine and told me how they'd sing together. Would you ask her if she would be willing to play some of Jackson's favorite songs?"

"It would be my pleasure."

Tears rolled down my cheeks, and we shared our sorrow.

Kai wanted to go with Caitlin and me to see Catherine. She was in the parlor between lessons and was knitting in her chair. "Well, hello Caitlin, who have you drug in with you!" She knew our footsteps and our smells.

Caitlin put her arms around Catherine, and I said, "We have sad news, Jackson died during *Montebello's* launch."

Her voice caught, and her face took on a distant look, "Oh my, I was deeply concerned when I learned about the launch accident. I'm so sorry!"

Caitlin said, "Mildred has arranged the funeral for Saturday and asked if you'd play during the service."

"Of course, it would be an honor."

"We'll pick you up at nine in the morning, and I'll contact your students to reschedule their lessons."

"Thank you, Caitlin."

Catherine reached out and said, "Kai, take my hand."

He looked at me and then hesitantly took her hand.

She squeezed it and said, "Please tell me what happened?"

Since the accident, Kai had hardly spoken, but he slowly recounted the events with Catherine. When he said, "I had to walk over dead bodies. Th..th..the..ah..ah," he began speaking in Mandarin, then stopped in mid-sentence, looked at me, and started sweating profusely.

Visibly saddened, Catherine softly said, "Kai, it's okay to grieve. You've been through a horrific accident. I know all of you had a special relationship with Jackson, and at a time like this, it helps to be with those you love and to share memories."

Kai pulled away, and Catherine extended her hand to me as she said, "Jackson loved to sing. He'd ask me to play his favorite hymns, and he sang along off-key as I played, but it didn't matter to him or me. I know the songs he loved, so I will play them at the service as my gift."

"He changed our lives, helped us escape from the logging camp, brought us to Collingwood, and got us jobs. He was special, and I miss him so much," I said.

Kai's blurted, "There were many s..s..slurs and s..s..slights he encountered at the s..s..shipyard, but he never retaliated. He was kindhearted and encouraging."

∽

There were about forty people in the church to pay their respects at the funeral. To open the service, Catherine played soft classical music, and Pastor Jones spoke of what a good person Jackson was, extending himself to help others in need with joy in his heart and a broad smile on his face. Catherine played his favorite hymns, and the congregation sang.

After the Pastor's message, I looked down at him in the coffin, and a chill washed over me. I played Jackson's song from the train on the xiao while Caitlin sang:

> *I'm a man of heroic deeds.*
> *I'm a man with pride and dignity.*
> *I endured the separation from my mother.*
> *Drifting on a voyage of thousands of miles.*
> *Sorrow is to be so far away from home.*

Then I said to him, "My brother, now you're at home with your mother." My eyes burned and tears streamed down my cheeks. Caitlin put her arm around me, and the Coffey sisters embraced us.

Mildred wailed throughout the service, especially when the wooden box was closed. I couldn't imagine her grief, seeing her beloved in the casket. I regretted not preparing his body for burial, dressing and shaving him because I didn't want him to be touched by anyone who held prejudice against him. Unfortunately, while I was involved with Joseph's funeral, his body was taken to the mortuary and embalmed. It would've been special for me to be the last person to care for him.

Caitlin and Wei Lei helped serve refreshments, then we drove twenty miles out of town to bury him in the Negro cemetery.

On the drive home, I said to Catherine, "I went to my grandmother's funeral in China. It was a solemn ceremony like the one for Joseph. I have never seen people wail at a service like today, even those who didn't know Jackson."

"People cope with death differently. You need to consider their culture and family background. There is no right way to express sorrow."

I looked at Kai, whose eyes were bloodshot. He said, "I was torn up seeing Mildred break down."

I put my arm on his shoulder and said, "They were so happy discussing wedding plans."

"I can't imagine what it's like for Mildred. She kept repeating that she felt cheated," Caitlin said as she reached from the back seat and squeezed my arm.

"He never said anything hurtful to anyone and did what was asked of him without complaint. He was never treated right by the bosses at the shipyard. I have to get out of there," Kai lamented.

Catherine said, "Jackson had his self-respect. He earned his freedom, worked for everything he had, and never let others determine how he measured his life."

"It ought to have been me and not Jackson," Kai whispered.

"I feel bad for Mildred, but I'm glad you're still here," Wei Lei said as she patted him on the shoulder.

"Despite all of this, you have to choose to be thankful for Jackson's life," Catherine said.

"Kai, remember when you tried to open the bottle of pop with your teeth, I can still hear Jackson laughing," I said.

We all laughed when Catherine said, "Open a pop bottle with your teeth!"

∽

Later in the week, I read the following article in the *Collingwood Sentinel*:

> *The shipbuilding industry has played an essential role in Collingwood's economy since the early 1900s. In the past decade, it has employed nearly 2,000 people in a town of 8,000. With support services, one in three individuals earn their livelihood from the shipyard, and it pays the best wages in town.*

> *The Simco Shipbuilding Company is a fascinating place, and the launches are spectacular. This year's launch day for Montebello arrived on the first Thursday in May. The shipyard whistle routinely blew three times a day, at eight to start work, at noon for a lunch break, and at five to signal the end of the day shift. The whistle was a comforting sound to the town as it meant all was normal, and there was work at the shipyard. The crowd was waiting anxiously, and the dignitaries and special guests were streaming in to watch the launch when the whistle blew at 11:35 a.m., twenty-five minutes before the scheduled noon launch.*

I thought of what I saw that day, then put the paper in the fireplace and lit a match.

Chapter Six

1963

Julian turned inward after Joseph's death, complained of pain, lost his appetite, and had trouble falling and staying asleep. He repeatedly spoke of loving his son despite their arguments and estrangement.

When Taylor arrived at the house for their regular weekly meeting, I greeted him, and he didn't say a word or make eye contact with me. I led him into Julian's office and turned to leave when Julian said, "Winson, I want you to stay."

After I sat down, he said to Taylor, "This will be the last time I meet with you regularly. From this time forward, Winson will be my intermediary for any activities at the bank, and he's to have full access to all areas."

I was surprised as I adjusted my posture, and when I looked at Taylor, he straightened his back, pulled on his tie, and continued to avoid making eye contact with me. "I must object. He's a foreigner, a Chinaman. Our customers won't want to be served by his kind."

"Winson will represent my interests, and I insist you treat him as if he were me. And call him by his proper name. He is a legal Canadian citizen."

Taylor cast a disdainful glance at me, then returned to lock stares with Julian, like bulls facing off against one another. "I understand that he will be a runner for correspondence, but he shouldn't have access to the vault and cash drawers." He paused, waiting for a reaction.

"He works for me. Why shouldn't he have access to the vault?" Julian was pulling energy from somewhere, and I didn't expect it to last, given his lack of sleep and appetite.

Taylor looked me up and down, and one side of his upper lip pulled upwards as he replied, "Let me explain my reasoning. If he were to have access to those areas, and if there was an audit, he'd need to be present at the bank and, at the same time, if you needed him to be available for your personal needs at home, this would be problematic. In addition to the pragmatic reason: we have access protocols that have been in place for years."

"I hear your arguments and accept that condition for the time being."

Sitting back in his chair, Taylor smirked as though he had won the first round of a fight.

Julian added, "I want him to have access to my personal safe-deposit box. On another issue, I want you to scrutinize who you do business with at the bank."

He clenched his armrests and said, "What are you referring to?"

"Have you opened an account for Imperial Lumber Company?"

Taylor gave me a demeaning look and then turned back to Julian. "They're a lumber supplier and are selling wood to Drott's."

"Do they have a tax identification number?" Julian asked.

"I'm sure they do, but I'll have to check." He nodded curtly as if expecting the matter to be forgotten.

"Ask them to close their account if they don't."

Taylor stood up abruptly, straightened his suit, and said, "Imperial Lumber is a new business in this area but has operated in British Columbia for a long time. After your accident, I have run the bank at a profit and have been responsible for generating new business. Although we have done very well, we can't afford to turn down new business."

He leaned in toward Julian and firmly said, "You know I want to take over the bank one day."

"I appreciate your efforts, but I want to remain involved and want Winson involved. I also need to know more about Imperial Lumber and the owners. Send me a memo of whatever information you have."

Taylor glared at Julian. "Is there anything else, Sir?"

"Yes, I want you to show Winson more respect than I have witnessed today, and I believe you owe him an apology. You may return to the bank."

Taylor turned his back to Julian and left without looking at me.

⤼

Julian demanded more pain pills, was disinterested most of the day and lost his taste for most foods. I suggested trying different diets to which Rhoda objected, preferring routine.

One morning I awoke early and prepared congee. When Rhoda entered the kitchen and saw me, she thundered, "What are you doing in the kitchen, and what's this?"

"Chinese porridge called congee. I wanted to try a different breakfast for Julian. If he doesn't like it, you can prepare his normal breakfast. I made extra for you to try."

Her mouth pulled to the left, and she made a face as she took a spoonful, but after taking a second portion, she said, "This is pretty good."

When I took it to Julian, he frowned and said, "I'm not hungry."

"I woke before sunrise this morning to make you a special dish from China. Try one bite."

He furrowed his brow but didn't object as I put a spoonful in his mouth. He rolled it around, looked at me, and smiled, "It's good!"

He ate three-quarters of the bowl, which was a significant improvement. When I took the dishes back to the kitchen, Rhoda grabbed the bowl, before I cleaned it. Her mouth opened wide, but for once, no sound came out. Moments of silence were broken by her question. "Did you eat his congee?"

"It was all, Julian."

She narrowed her eyes and said, "Are you sure?"

"Adding a spoon of maple syrup helps."

She burst into laughter.

This was only a temporary respite to his despair.

He asked me to push him around the garden in the early afternoons, and one day said, "Ruthie loved this garden, and I have wonderful memories of holding her hand and walking around the yard, admiring the blooms and enjoying the fragrances. I seldom took time for the little things and was too preoccupied with business. If only we had left home later, or sooner, or taken a different route to the bank. She was my rock! We told each other we would be together for a thousand years."

To distract him, I stopped and cut some roses and held them up for Julian to smell. His lips curled into a momentary smile before he continued, "I'm tortured over what has happened. I tried to be available for Joseph, but he turned away, and now I'm without both of them. I survive one day at a time, but nothing seems to matter."

He paused and stared at the sky. "You and I come from different worlds, but time is the one thing that is the same for us. The years teach much that the days never knew."

The next afternoon, he asked me to take him to the lake, and he stared at the water and said he wished he could be with Ruthie again. Later that day, I told Virginia about Julian's behavior and conversations. With concern in her eyes, she said, "Julian has lost hope. He will be increasingly dependent on you for bank affairs because he wants to disengage."

Julian took less interest in the newspapers, even though I tried to read to him every day. He perked up one morning when I read newspapers from across Canada regarding the *Montebello* accident.

An Ottawa article said:

> The House of Commons initiated an investigation on the premature launch of the Montebello joined by the Department of Labor, Attorney General, Royal Canadian Mounted Police, and Ontario Workmen's Compensation Board.

A Toronto paper said:

> The Shipyard's Technical Department had been responsible for many successful side launches and has begun its investigation into the cause of the premature start.

An article from a Chicago newspaper was particularly interesting:

> *Simco Shipbuilding had been concerned about general business conditions the year before the Montebello launch. It had lobbied the Prime Minister and Parliament for more contracts and subsidies for the shipyard to avoid closing. In the weeks before the launch, the company began layoffs, and more were expected as there were no new ship contracts in the pipeline. This ship's hull was the largest launched to date, and the weight of the ship, greatly exceeded previous launches.*

The tragedy impacted all of us in some way. Julian lost Joseph, I lost Jackson, and Mildred lost her fiancé, and many families lost their husbands and fathers. It impacted business at the bank. Since most shipyard workers were married men with families, the transpiring events drastically changed their lives. Bank employees told me that the men who quit or lost their jobs had difficulty finding work, and the wives couldn't support their families because few positions were available for women.

For more than a year, the investigation continued with reviews of every aspect of the launch. Julian said that insurance adjusters focused on the shipbuilding company for acts of gross negligence or mismanagement. If the issue was mechanical or material defects or miscalculated engineering specifications, the burden of responsibility would fall directly on Simco Shipbuilding, and the company couldn't stay solvent if they were held liable, which could lead to a bankruptcy declaration.

The City didn't want the shipyard to declare bankruptcy or close because it would be an economic catastrophe for the area. Simco and the City were aligned and needed a scapegoat.

A likely candidate to be charged with the failure was Caitlin's father, the launch manager. Mulroney's job was to signal the start of the launch, and a theory was that he might've given the signal prematurely. Caitlin told me his actions on the day of the launch were questioned and reviewed several times. He was quoted in newspaper articles, saying that his procedures followed the routine as all previous launches, all of which transpired without incident and that he never signaled the start of the launch. Inspectors' repeatedly questioned his pre-launch operations and procedures and concluded that Mulroney was responsible for the premature launch, and he was terminated without benefits.

Caitlin was still in contact with her mother, who told Caitlin that after the report's findings were announced, their friends abandoned them, and Mulroney had turned to alcohol.

One evening after putting Julian to bed, I looked forward to enjoying dinner with Caitlin. After she placed food on the table, I pulled out her chair, seated her, and kissed her on the cheek. "Sweetheart, the food looks and smells delicious."

She just nodded and picked at her food. Her clothes, which highlighted her attractive figure, now seemed to hang loose on her body. I search her face, then asked, "How was your day?"

With a disconcerted look, she replied, "I spent time with Mum today. She has fewer odd jobs, Daddy can't find work, and no one offers help. Even the church cut off the food they had been providing. I have never seen her so distraught."

"I'm sorry to hear about what they're going through." I didn't know what else to say, so we ate in silence. Then she went upstairs to read while I checked on Julian. When I entered the bedroom, she was already asleep.

When I woke early the next morning, Caitlin's place in bed was empty. I found her asleep on the sofa. I prepared hot tea, toast, and jam, placed a rose in a small vase, carried them to her on a tray, put them on the coffee table, and looked at her, still asleep. She was the prettiest woman I'd ever seen! I was sad to see her distressed over her parents, but this was difficult because I was emotional over my history with her father. When she opened her eyes and saw me, she smiled.

"Good morning, my love. I'm sorry if you had a bad night," I said.

"It was the same restless night I've had over the past few weeks. My mind is too active." She looked tired as she sipped tea.

"Mum is desperate. They're barely holding on with what money they have, and all Daddy does is drink. Mum says he repeatedly recounts all his actions and is adamant he didn't conduct the launch processes different from previous ones. He's given up trying to find an answer."

She wrapped her arms around herself, her head dropped, and then with quivering lips she looked up at me and said, "Isn't there anything we can do to help?"

I remembered how hard Mulroney made it for me when he found out Caitlin and I were dating. He had me followed, sent thugs to threaten me, planned an ambush, then beat me close to death. Only with Julian's intervention and the threat of court action against Simco Shipbuilding did he cease. For all I knew, he was the reason Jay was still following me.

Her hand slipped into mine, and when she looked at me, her deep blue eyes pierced my heart as she said, "I know how bad Daddy hurt you. Hurt us."

"It's a miracle we're together. You remember how I didn't want to expose you to the abuse I was sure would come if we got married, not only from your father and his cronies but from others who'd feel the same way towards a mixed marriage."

"Hate and fear come from ignorance. Daddy didn't know you, but they're my parents, and I know you can help them find answers that Daddy can't."

The mention of helping her father irritated and repulsed me. "I need to check on Julian. Can we talk about this later?"

"Whenever you're ready."

The morning went quickly as I conducted my regular routine with Julian. After lunch, Julian took a nap, and I let Rhoda know I was going to take a walk in the backyard. I sat on the bench where Caitlin and I used to meet by the blue spruce. It was difficult, if not impossible, for me to consider opening myself to what Caitlin asked. How could I forgive Mulroney? It would be like my absolving Dung and Tak.

I needed to think, not react. YeYe taught me when stressed to close my eyes, quiet my mind and emotions, concentrate on breathing to detach myself, step away from my circumstances, and see myself from a distance.

With eyes closed, I slowed my breathing, put my hand over YeYe's ivory medallion around my neck, and let my subconscious take me to another place until everything became quiet and peaceful.

Then I saw someone approach but couldn't make out who. When the figure walked toward me in a measured way, a chill shook my entire body, followed by a warm sensation. I couldn't move, yet I didn't want to move.

As the figure drew closer, it looked familiar. Closer yet, it resembled YeYe, but that was impossible. When I saw his eyes, I trembled. It was YeYe!

With those strong hands, he pulled me close, and his warmth enveloped me. I was too choked up to say anything and only wanted to remain in his embrace.

I finally whispered in his ear, "YeYe, you know I didn't want to leave home, leave you, Mother and Lijuan. I wanted to be with you and take care of you."

"My son, it's okay. I know your heart. You had to go."

My heart pounded, and I was too emotional to speak. YeYe's hands clutched my upper arms, and he waited until I settled down. He put his finger to his lips, then mine, and looked deep into my eyes, which was his way of sharing his peace to calm my anxiety.

"You are in my heart, and you have never left me, nor have I left you. I am not walking on the earth any longer, and I can only be with you a little while."

"YeYe, I want to be where you are."

"I am always with you, by your side, in the sky, in the wind that blows through the trees. When you play the xiao, I play with you."

I struggled to understand what was taking place but knew the calm that came over me was from him. His appearance was youthful and his walk was bouncy. When I looked at his skin, it had no wrinkles or spots, and his voice was soft and without its raspiness.

"Do you remember Yuan?" he asked.

I hadn't thought of him in years. "How do you know about him?"

"It's immaterial. Do you remember when you nursed him back to health?"

"How do you…"

He put his finger to my lips.

"Now stop and listen. There were reasons for Yuan's behavior, but you looked past his actions to help someone who was hurting and in dire need. You made a choice.

"When you look into Caitlin's heart, there is hurt for her parents. Yet she looks past how they treated both of you. What you did for Yuan is small in comparison to what you can do for Caitlin. When you help her parents, you help her. "Remember when we threw rocks into the water?"

I nodded.

"The ripples on one side of the pond became greater when they reached the other side. What you do for Caitlin's parents will magnify in your life. Again, you have a choice to make."

Questions flooded my mind. "YeYe, what happened to you? To Mother and Father? To Lijuan?"

"My son, I must leave now, but remember, I am with you always."

"Don't go! Please stay. I want to be with you again. Look, I kept your medallion safe to return to you."

He reached out, put his hand on the leather strap around my neck, rubbed it with his fingers, looked at me with a sparkle in his eyes, and said, "I will always be with you."

Then he put his finger to his lips, then to mine. "Remember, allow yourself to be who you were created to be."

He bowed to me. I was in shock because out of respect, I was never to let him bow to me first, and my bow must be lower than his. This wasn't to be done.

He rose, looked at me, which was his way of expressing his deep love and respect for me, backed away with his eyes on me, and then turned and moved toward a distant figure who waved with a familiar gesture. It was NaiNai, but she was no longer bent over.

When I opened my eyes, they were gone, and I was still sitting on the bench.

Could it be that as our bodies age and faculties dull, what is inside never tires, never ages, never changes?

Are our spirits eternal?

I kept this experience to myself and didn't tell Caitlin.

Chapter Seven

The wind howled, the sky was grey, and days were getting shorter. It was late fall, and I was on my way to the bank to deliver loan documents from Julian. When I turned the corner on Main Street, a man in an old overcoat, with his hat pulled low on his forehead, ambled toward me.

He looked familiar, and I considered greeting him, but when I looked around and saw many out-of-work shipyard employees loitering along storefronts staring at me, I felt uncomfortable. I had developed a protective instinct to avoid eye contact, which I learned from years of prejudice. Caitlin encouraged me to change this behavior, so I reconsidered and said to the man in the overcoat, "Good day, eh."

He barely looked up as we both paused. I extended my hand, and our eyes met. His icy blue eyes were familiar. Where had I seen this man? I seldom failed to remember a face, and it took me a moment before I realized it was Caitlin's father.

We were silent as we stood facing one another, shaking hands. On edge, I took a step back, but when Mulroney gave a slight nod of acknowledgment, I returned it. It was the first subtle acknowledgment I ever received from him. I was flooded with conflicting emotions, this man rejected my marriage, yet now he was in deep despair.

He lowered his head when he looked at me and muttered, "I'm sorry. I was wrong. Can you ever forgive me?"

Mulroney sent thugs to mock, beat, and urinate on me, and he persecuted Jackson, Kai, and even his daughter, and now he was asking for forgiveness. His plea was out of desperation.

Why should I respond? If he respected me as an equal, he should anticipate revenge. I wanted to be anywhere else, but not standing in front of him.

My mind raced. What response would Caitlin and YeYe want from me? Then I remembered what Catherine told me after I was beaten, 'Not to dwell on the past, nor the pain consuming me, live for the present and the future, take the path which leads to freedom.'

Julian had said, 'Nobody can get away with anything. There are always consequences.' If I forgave him, would it allow me to let go of my pain?

My thoughts were interrupted as Mulroney slurred, "How could you have peace during the times I sent the boys after you? I hated and admired you at the same time."

His eyes met mine, then he looked down and said, "Please forgive me."

He said he was wrong and asked for forgiveness, but can a venomous snake change its nature?

I lost Jackson, Julian lost Joseph, there had been enough distress and pain. My heart had been pecked at like a chick trying to hatch out of its shell. "I forgive you." Anxiety flooded my body, and before I lost my composure, I said, "I'm late and have to go."

Later, when I was with Caitlin, I told her about the encounter with her father. Since our wedding, she hadn't seen much of her parents. "Your father was slumped over, his face was gaunt, and he looked to have aged more than his years."

"Mum told me ever since Daddy was blamed for the accident, he drinks more often. He has always been a drinker and often said, 'God gave whiskey to the Irish to keep them from taking over the world.'"

"You haven't told me much about your family."

"Daddy's family immigrated to Canada from Dublin, along with many others, during the Irish potato famine. He said they faced severe hardship in Nova Scotia and with so many Irish immigrants, many signs read, 'No Irish Need Apply.' His family struggled to survive, and his father became an alcoholic. Daddy was the oldest of eight children, and at ten years old, his father sent him to live with his older brother, who drank whiskey at breakfast and cursed incessantly. He won't talk about life with his uncle and Daddy never returned to school nor spoke to his father or mother again.

"Mum was also from a poor Irish immigrant family and when she met Daddy, they were both looking for a change in their lives. She was attracted to his blue eyes and physique and said he had a hothead, a cold heart, and an Irish temper. They eloped and moved west to Collingwood, where Daddy found a job at the shipbuilding company. Building ships was his life, and he worked his way up to launch manager until the *Montebello*."

When tears rolled down her cheeks, I gently pulled her into my arms. She trembled as she tried to speak, so I put my finger to my lips, then to hers. "Everything will be okay. With Julian's help, I'll try to find out what was behind the accident. Do you want to invite your parents to meet with us?"

She held me tight and whispered, "Thank you."

I hoped mother and daughter could be close again, and it might happen as Caitlin arranged for us to meet for dinner at their home. When I thought about Mulroney encountering discrimination from the community because of the accident and issues with his father, I realized we had some common background, whether he recognized it or not.

Julian had questions about the accident that killed Joseph, and I needed his help. The next morning I told him of my conversation with Caitlin and Mulroney's apology. Then we brainstormed different areas to investigate and why Mulroney would be targeted as a scapegoat.

Julian said, "Rumors have circulated through town that yard workers were pressured not to speak about what caused the launch accident. If the shipyard closed, they'd lose their jobs, and it would devastate their families, suppliers would shut down, eventually the grain elevators, and then the railroad. I'm willing to help because Joseph died, and I want answers. But we might not like what we discover."

✎

It had been a long time since I wanted a cigarette, but as we approached the one-story wood-frame home with an extended front porch and two Red Maples in the front yard, my urge to smoke was strong. We climbed the steps holding hands, and as Caitlin rang the doorbell, I had a lump in my throat, not knowing what to expect.

When Caitlin's mother opened the door, she hugged Caitlin, then extended her hand to me and said, "Hello Winson, it's so nice to meet you. Please call me Maureen."

Mulroney came from behind her, kissed Caitlin on the cheek, and then extended his hand. "Please come in, Winson, welcome to our home, and call me Kierian." He wore khaki pants, a long-sleeved white shirt and looked smaller than how I remembered him from the yard.

Maureen added, "Please do come in and make yourself at home. I'm glad you've made my daughter happy." She looked drawn, spoke in a high voice, wore a mid-length, blue floral cotton dress with short sleeves, and her hair was reddish-brown with grey streaks.

Caitlin was squeezing my left hand, but I needed to let go as Maureen reached out and hugged me in an awkward embrace.

"Mum, those daisies are beautiful. Where did you get them?" Caitlin asked as she pointed to a bouquet on the entry table.

I thought she was trying to distract her parents to help me relax.

"From our friend Sandy. She has the most beautiful garden." She kept glancing at Kierian and then said, "Caitlin, come help me in the kitchen and let the men talk."

"Of course." She flashed a smile at me, then followed her mother.

Kierian and I sat in the parlor in two chairs separated by a simple wood table and a lamp with an ivory shade trimmed with gold fringe. There were uneasy minutes of silence until he caught my eye and said, "Again, I want to apologize for my actions. I was angry and wanted to send a message. I have no excuse and am ashamed of my actions. I wasn't man enough to talk to you myself."

"I accept your apology."

His eyes were darting about, as he asked, "Do you want a cigarette?"

I hadn't smoked since working for Julian, but at that moment, I wanted one in the worst way and said, "Please."

He pulled a pack from his pocket, tapped it for one to slide out, and leaned it toward me. After I took one, he pulled another out, ignited his lighter, and lit mine, then his. I never envisioned sitting in his parlor smoking together.

"Maureen told me you left your family to flee a communist government in China."

"Yes. None of us have a choice where or when we're born or what we look like. Those are circumstances beyond our control." I didn't want to discuss my background, so I added, "We all seek a better life."

He looked at me with an expression of surprise. "Well said."

"I understand you were blamed for the accident and can't find other work."

As he nodded, I flinched, remembering my difficulties finding a job.

"I lost a close friend, and Mr. LeBlanc lost his son. Both of us want to know more about the accident. My friend Kai works at the yard, and he said many of the launch way timbers were used on prior launches." Without thinking, I added, "Kai said our friend Jackson was driving out the dogs that day. He didn't make it. He was one of my best friends."

He started fidgeting and lit another cigarette before the first one was out. The pained expression on his face told me that he thought I knew about how Jackson was mistreated in the yard. I didn't want the conversation to get emotional, so I asked, "Tell me about the weeks before the launch and the steps you followed up to and during the launch."

He took a deep drag, then spoke slowly, "I have gone over what we did hundreds of times. We went through the same procedures as every prior launch. That morning we had a team that worked beneath the ship for four hours, hammering wedges between the blocks under the ship, which raised the ship onto the launchways. They were putting the final wedges in place when she started to groan, and then all hell broke loose as she moved."

He looked away and took several dry swallows. "This was my ninth launch as manager. All the procedures looked proper, and the construction of the launchways was according to plan. Nothing was awry in the procedures my department controlled. I thought there must be factors we overlooked, if not in the process, perhaps in the engineering or the materials used to support the *Montebello* before the launch, but I had no control over the engineering or design of the launch structure. Maybe there were miscalculations in the materials or sizing.

"I know I didn't signal the launch because the crew was still knocking out the wedges, or as you said, 'Driving out the dogs' when the ship started sliding. There has always been enough time between knocking out the wedges and signaling the ax men to cut the lines for the men with sledgehammers to get out from under the ship."

"I was told *Montebello* weighed much more than all previous ships. Did management add to the launch infrastructure?

"As far as I know, specifications were identical to previous launches, except that the dock was extended to accommodate the length of the ship, and the engines were installed before the launch because they were too heavy for the cranes to lift after she was in the water."

"I spent almost three years at a logging camp outside of Vancouver differentiating between wood types, testing timbers to determine if they were robust or rotten. What if there was a failure in the timbers used for the launchways or butter boards, even the wedges, could defective wood have contributed to the sudden ship movement?"

"I don't know, that's a possibility. Management laid-off workers weeks before the launch because there was no new ship to build, and if they were laying off workers to save money, they could've also cut corners with materials or in other areas. I sure want to know what caused her to move when she did."

"Do you know what they did with the timbers from the launch?"

"They should be in the scrap yard."

"Can we inspect them?"

"I can't get into the yard anymore. Do you think Mr. LeBlanc could help get us access?"

Caitlin interrupted by asking us to come for dinner. When we sat, Kierian said, "Winson and I are going to investigate the launch. We want to examine the timbers."

When he used the word 'we' and called me by my name, it felt strange.

On the way home, Caitlin took my hand as we walked down the steps and crossed the street. Before entering Julian's house, she put her head on my shoulder and whispered, "I don't think I told you that my father's name, Kierian, is Gaelic and means, little dark one."

Extraordinary the way life works at times.

Chapter Eight

The next morning, I spoke to Julian about the time with Caitlin's family and the ideas for investigating the *Montebello* accident. The last year had been difficult for Julian, and I hoped getting involved in the investigation would give him focus and divert attention from his despair.

"Do you know who I could contact to inspect the old timbers used in the launch?" I asked.

"Let's make a few calls."

Two days later, Julian's friend quietly arranged for a crew chief named Danny to escort Kierian and me through the scrap pile.

When we met him, he took us off to a corner of the yard, looked around, and with no one near, said in a low voice, "What questions do you have?"

"According to your procedures, how often can the timbers be reused?" I asked.

"They're normally replaced every third launch. We were way past the third on some of the wood, but the head office told us to reuse the materials after they were inspected and certified."

As we looked through the timbers, I noted many weren't just broken but rotted. I took an axe and struck a number of them, and many crumbled on the first blow. Julian sent a camera with me, so we took photographs of the wood, the good and the bad.

"It looks like these boards were used on more than three launches," I commented.

"You're correct. Some were used on up to ten launches," Danny replied.

"How were these boards approved to be used?"

"I wasn't involved with the inspection. There was a third-party inspection official from Ottawa who looked at the wood and was accompanied by Tom Adams, Simco's Chief Financial Officer."

When we got back to the car, I said to Kierian, "It looks like many of those timbers were rotted before the launch. A qualified inspector wouldn't approve them for use in a ship launch."

"Everyone knew the company was going through a difficult period and weeks before the launch, the company started laying off essential workers, not only in my division but also in other areas. I told them they were furloughing my best workers and keeping the dregs. Management cut back everywhere, but I hadn't considered the possibility of their using defective wood to reduce costs."

"Could there have been a payoff to the inspector to look the other way?"

Kierian shrugged his shoulders.

"I will talk to Mr. LeBlanc for his thoughts on the best way to proceed. Let's get these photographs developed as evidence."

Chapter Nine

Julian gave me additional responsibilities at the bank. Late on a Friday afternoon, I went to the bank to return documents and gather others for Julian to review. When I walked into the file room, Cheek and Taylor were discussing the pledge of bonds from the Iron Ore Company of Canada, as collateral for a loan to a Toronto businessman named Roger Compton. When they saw me, they stopped their conversation and gave me a hard penetrating look.

"What do you want?" Taylor asked.

"I'm here to pull some files."

"Shouldn't you be at the mansion to clean up after the old man?" he asked.

Cheek looked over at Taylor and sneered, "I wouldn't let a stinking chink touch my privates." He then turned his balding head back towards me, and his pasty face lost all expression. I could taste his hate and smell the stench of his breath reeking of alcohol as he took a step closer to me but was held back by his rather large stomach. He quickly raised his hands, and I flinched because I thought he was going to hit me. Instead, he took the lapels of my jacket between his thumbs and fingers, softly feeling the quality of the fabric. He leaned in so that his face was just inches from mine, his pale gray eyes bloodshot and crusted in the corners. With a laugh, he said, "Are you still wearing the cripple's clothes?" His spittle struck me in the face and made me want to vomit.

I felt he was a hair-trigger from exploding if I as much uttered a word, so I took a step back, trying to establish some distance.

Then Taylor stuck his finger in my face, "Get about your business and get out of here. We're busy. Besides, you smell like shit from the food you eat!"

"I'll bet he's still using pigeon blood on his food." Cheek said as Taylor laughed.

"What's pigeon blood?" I snapped.

"It's shit sauce, that's why you smell the way you do," Cheek bristled.

I forced myself not to respond to their taunting, even though I was livid inside. They were often rude to me, but never this ugly.

"Go back to your nursing duties!" Taylor demanded.

I gathered the information Julian wanted and started to walk away when Taylor grabbed the files, thumbed through them, and said, "These files are restricted. I can have you fired."

"We caught him," Cheek shouted.

"These files are what Mr. LeBlanc requested." I felt the pressure building inside me, so I looked away at nothing in particular, trying to remain calm even though I was wound tight.

"We'll see about that," Taylor said as he handed the files to Cheek.

Cheek mockingly said, "Every disease we have comes from China. Why don't you get the fuck out of our country, you piece of Chinese shit."

"I'm here on Mr. LeBlanc's behalf, and you know it. He's not going to be happy when I show up without those files."

I started to walk out of the file room when Taylor called me back, and Cheek threw the files toward me. The files landed on the floor, and they watched me pick them up. When I walked through the lobby, I felt all the employees watching me as I left the bank.

Taylor and Cheek's arrogance was like Dung and Tak. I balled my fists and wanted to break something but suppressed my anger. Their mocking and insolence made me suspicious of everything concerning them. I tried to clear my mind, but then I saw Jay waiting across the street.

I walked up to him, stood a few feet away, and stared face to face. He had pinpoint pupils, and his eyes were bloodshot. "Did Taylor hire you to follow me?"

He looked away, put a cigarette to his lips, took a drag, then turned toward me and blew smoke. I wanted an answer, but I looked around and saw several men watching us, so I decided to head home, fuming inside.

When I returned to Julian's, I asked him about Iron Ore bonds and told him I overheard Taylor and Cheek discussing a loan secured by those bonds.

"That's strange. Several years ago, there was a merger between Hanna Company and Iron Ore Company of Canada. The IOC bondholders turned in their bonds and were issued new bond certificates in Hanna." Julian raised his eyebrows. "Who was the loan made to?"

"Roger Compton with Adolph Enterprises."

"I know Adolph Enterprises and its founder, Wendell Compton. He was a good businessman, and when he died about six years ago, his son, Roger, took over the business, but he's a womanizer and never worked a full day in his life.

Humph." He looked up at the ceiling like he often did when he was in profound thought.

"It's too late to do anything today. On Monday, go to the bank, pull the Compton loan files, the loan documents, and payment history. Let's review them. Also, check to see if the Imperial Lumber account was closed. Taylor has not provided me an update."

"I think I should go when Taylor and Cheek are at lunch. Taylor pulled the files from me today and said I wasn't authorized to have them and could get fired. He also said he's having me followed. I've noticed a man following me for some time, and he was waiting for me outside the bank just now. You might have noticed him across the street from time to time."

"What! Something's going on, and I don't like it. Get Taylor on the phone." As I turned to get the phone, he said, "No, wait. I want to review the Compton files before I confront him."

∽

When I returned from the bank on Monday, I took Julian to his office and put the documents on the easel.

"Here is the original loan, made five years ago to Roger Compton. He pledged Iron Ore bonds to secure capital to expand Adolph Enterprises. Additional loans were made to Compton, secured by bonds from Canadian Pacific Railroad.

"Here is the *New and Renewed Loan Report* for Compton. The bank renewed the earliest loans and then issued new loans in progressively higher amounts, still collateralized with bonds from Iron Ore and Canadian Pacific. The report shows the dollar amounts and the loan balances at the end of last month."

"Winson, this report doesn't mention Hannah Corporation. I don't want to believe that Taylor would do something illegal, but this is potential evidence to the contrary. Call Clive and ask him to come here and meet with us."

While we were waiting for Clive, Julian asked, "What about Imperial Lumber?"

"The account is open, and there have been limited transactions, no loans."

"Doing business with lawbreakers is never good," Julian said.

When Clive arrived, Rhoda brought him into the office. He was a middle-aged man with thick glasses and a mop of curly dark hair, wearing dark brown slacks with an open-collared shirt and tan jacket. He went directly to Julian, who looked up, smiled, and said, "Clive, thank you for coming so quickly. I would like to introduce you to my assistant Winson."

Clive faced me and extended his hand. "Finally, we meet. It's my pleasure."

"A pleasure to meet you, Mr. Owen."

"Please, call me Clive." I smiled and nodded.

Julian asked Clive to sit at his desk. I had set out the files for his review. He studied the documents, and when he had turned the last page, he removed his glasses, leaned back in the chair, and said, "How did you discover these?"

I repeated what I had told Julian.

Julian looked pensive, as if expecting bad news, then said, "Clive, what do you make of this?"

"Bond certificates in Iron Ore should have been tendered to the transfer agent and replaced with certificates in Hannah Corporation after the merger consummated. There is no mention of Hannah in these reports. If the posted bonds are illegitimate collateral, that would be evidence of malfeasance, and embezzlement may have been committed. We would need evidence that Taylor intentionally misappropriated bank loan proceeds. We need to inspect the certificates in the bank's vault."

Clive paused as if to measure Julian's reaction, then asked, "Julian, have you observed any peculiar behavior from Taylor or Cheek?"

"Taylor took some files away from Winson Friday afternoon and told him he could be fired for taking them from the bank. He also told Winson he is having him followed. I wanted to call Taylor Friday but decided to wait until we reviewed the loan documents. I don't like Taylor's behavior, and I've told him that Winson is my representative and authorized to do anything I ask of him."

Julian stared in the distance, then his eyes squinted shut, and he said in a soft tone, "After I lost Ruthie, nothing mattered. This was compounded by my physical problems and the narcotics I take for pain. I haven't had the necessary focus regarding bank affairs, and I think Taylor has taken advantage of his position because of my condition."

He cleared his throat and said firmly, "I stopped my weekly meetings with Taylor six months ago. The last time we met, I told Taylor that he was less transparent with me, and he said he didn't want to burden me with a loan or bank details after Joseph's death. I'm afraid I have been neglectful of my oversight responsibilities."

Clive replied, "Julian, don't be too hard on yourself." He gave Julian a smile that only would come from years of friendship.

Then he continued, "We need to verify that the certificates, which have been posted as collateral, are authentic. If they're counterfeit or missing, then the act was intentional and is the burden of proof we need to establish a case against Taylor and maybe Cheek. Let's deal with the bonds first. The answer to one problem may solve the other."

"Taylor told me he wants to buy the bank. If he is embezzling for the purchase, we should conduct an official audit."

"Julian, you have reasonable cause to investigate the collateral, and besides, it's best practice to conduct compliance checks regularly. If there is economic loss, we contact the Collingwood Police and the Ontario Provincial Police and let them advise us on steps for filing charges. Would you be up to going to the bank yourself because I don't think you should give the vault combination to Winson or me?"

"Clive, I need to speak with you privately. Winson, bring us some Scotch."

As I was leaving, I overheard Julian say, "What would the consequences be if..."

I went to the kitchen and brought back tumblers with ice and a bottle of Macallan Single Malt. When I returned, Julian said, "Winson, if we attempt to investigate this further and don't find malfeasance..." His voice trailed off. He looked away, then back at me. "We're stirring up a hornet's nest. If we accuse Taylor and Cheek and don't find..." He stopped again and stared into space. "There would be repercussions. As Clive said, we need hard evidence. Winson, are there any other events that you've witnessed?"

"When Joseph died, you sent me to the bank for his birth certificate. Taylor and Cheek were in the vault at the time, and I told Peggy Bailey, who oversees Safe Keeping, that you needed the certificate. She said to wait while she asked Taylor for permission for us to enter. I heard Taylor yelling at her, and she was shaking with tears in her eyes when she came out of the vault. She told me Taylor screamed that he was never to be disturbed in the vault. Minutes later, Taylor stormed out red-eyed, threw a file at me, and said he wasn't at your beck and call.

"Peggy was visibly upset, so the next afternoon I took her flowers and apologized for the stress caused by requesting the birth certificate. She had difficulty maintaining her composure and told me Taylor threatened to terminate her if she ever came into the vault again when he was inside.

"I tried to reassure her, and she told me Taylor and Cheek had intimidated her for years and didn't think they were following bank policy. When I asked what she meant, she said everyone who enters the vault must sign in on a journal, post the date and time of entry and exit, but they told her they're exempt and wouldn't be signing in or out. I didn't tell you at the time because you were distraught over Joseph."

Julian interrupted, "That's enough. We need hard evidence. Clive, contact the Collingwood Police, see what procedures we need to follow."

Clive made the call and then relayed his conversation with the Chief of Police. "The Chief will assign a detective to open a file and initiate a secret investigation to determine if theft or fraud crimes have occurred against the bank. He said we need to conduct an internal audit to determine if the collateral is sufficient to support the loans and any losses. Let's discuss strategy before conducting an audit."

Julian had me call Peggy to find out the next scheduled bank examination. It was scheduled for the first Tuesday of the month, so he asked her to be sure the examiners saw all of the vault's collateral files, especially the Compton files.

I waited until Wednesday afternoon to see Peggy when she was alone and asked, "Did the examiner review all the files?"

She looked pale, and her body quivered as she shook her head. She wouldn't look at me as she moved files around on her desk.

"What happened?" I asked.

"I set out all the Compton loan files at the end of the day on Monday, but Taylor came in early Tuesday morning and only had specific files available for the examiner to review. After the examiner left, Taylor questioned me about putting all the files out for the auditor. I got choked up, apologized, and told him I misunderstood his instructions. He called me stupid and then threatened to fire me immediately if I didn't follow his specific instructions again." She was trembling, and her eyes were darting.

"Mr. LeBlanc won't let that happen."

"Mr. Taylor said he'd make it difficult for me to ever find work in town. I can't afford to lose my job. I live with my invalid mother and can't be without a paycheck. This has made everything worse." She folded her arms and bit her lower lip.

"Let me reassure you that we will protect you." I had no authority to tell her this.

I hurried home to report to Julian, and he had me get Clive on the phone. Julian said, "I'm at the end of my patience with Taylor's callous attitude. It's evident that the examiner's review process isn't conducted at arm's length."

Clive replied, "Taylor's being deceptive, but we need material evidence to uncover any illicit activity."

"I agree. Let's call Peggy and ask her to meet us here after work today."

That afternoon, when Peggy came into Julian's office, he thanked her for coming and said, "Peggy, I know this situation isn't pleasant for you, and I want you to know that I will take care of you, no matter what happens. I will protect you from Taylor, so your job and reputation are secure."

Peggy seemed to melt into the chair.

Clive approached her, put his hand on her shoulder, and said, "Let me add to what Julian said by assuring you that we will support and defend you. Our next step is to run the risk of opening the sealed envelopes to determine if everything is in order, but now Taylor is on high alert, especially as it relates to you, Peggy. We need to find a time when Taylor and Cheek won't be at the bank. Can we reseal the envelopes without Taylor knowing?"

"I have an old seal we can use. Mr. Taylor and Mr. Cheek usually take long lunches at the country club on Fridays. They often take customers to play golf and never return to the bank. Mr. LeBlanc, what if you and Winson meet me on Friday as soon as they leave for lunch?"

"If I go to the bank, it will arouse too much attention, and Taylor and Cheek will find out I was there. I can give my combination to Winson, and you can put in your combination. Clive, you should be there as a witness."

Clive replied, "I'll bring my Polaroid camera to record what we discover."

"I can lock the door to the basement while we're in the vault," Peggy added.

∞

I met Clive at the bank on Friday. As we talked at the top of the staircase that led down to the basement, I saw a man, wearing a dark grey pinstripe suit and carrying a black briefcase, walk into the bank. It was Tak. I had not seen him since he demanded $1,000 from Kai and me.

My chest felt like it was about to explode. Was Tak meeting Taylor and Cheek? Had they momentarily stepped out, and were they about to return to meet Tak? How would Clive and I explain why we were together at the bank if we were confronted by Taylor?

Clive saw the expression on my face and motioned me to move down the stairs. I turned and saw Peggy pacing at the bottom of the staircase.

Clive whispered, "Did you see Taylor?"

"No, it's Tak. What should we do?"

"Go down to Peggy and close the door to Safe Keeping. Tak doesn't know me. I'll watch for Taylor, and if it's clear, I'll knock on the door twice. If I don't knock in ten minutes, I'll have left the bank. Reopen the door, go back to Julian's, and we'll regroup."

Before taking a step, I looked past Clive toward Tak, who now was looking straight at me. I know I reacted because when Tak caught my eyes, he nodded, touched his temple with his hand, and doffed a wave toward me. Was everything falling apart before my eyes?

I took the stairs and explained the situation to Peggy. I expected she might crumble, but she quietly locked the door, and we waited. I paced back and forth, my mind whirled thinking of Tak and Dung and the extensiveness of their network. Ten minutes seemed like an hour.

We heard two knocks on the door. Peggy looked agitated as if she didn't know what to expect when she unlocked the door. Clive was alone, and after Peggy closed the door, he said, "Tak made a deposit and left. Let's get to our business."

Peggy was shaking as we opened the vault and pulled five years of collateral files on Roger Compton. First, we opened the oldest active loans in sealed envelopes and found blank papers in them. Clive photographed each envelope before opening it, photographed the items inside, and took a photo of the resealed envelopes. He placed the morning newspaper on the table in the vault so that the date would be on the photos. The more recent envelopes had certificates amounting to $620,000 in various bonds. Peggy resealed the envelopes with wax, stamped them, then locked the vault. Clive and I each left at different times before Taylor or Cheek returned.

On my way out of the bank, a teller stopped me and handed me a folded note. I put it in my pocket and keep walking. I stopped before reaching Julian's and read the message. It was written in Mandarin, *'Now I know where you work. I'll arrange to meet you soon whether you want to or not.'* I couldn't worry about Tak with what was happening, nor did I want to tell Julian and add to his stress. It was a matter to deal with at a later time.

We took the photos to Julian, and Clive called the accounting firm he and Julian had used for years and asked them to review the loan files and photos.

Within a week, the accounting firm estimated the losses and made the following recommendations to Julian:

1. Notify the police of the losses.
2. Authenticate the bonds in the other loan envelopes.
3. Notify the bank's insurance carrier.

On Monday morning, before the bank opened, Clive and I met with Detective Inspector Oscar Hogan, from the Collingwood Police Department, two uniformed police officers, the lead accountant who reviewed the files, and two federal bank auditors from Ottawa in the parking lot behind the bank.

We all entered the bank together, and Clive called Taylor and Cheek into the conference room. Clive introduced Taylor and Cheek to everyone in the room.

Detective Inspector Hogan took over from there. "We're conducting an investigation and partial audit of bank records. We have reason to believe that improprieties may have occurred."

All the blood left Taylor and Cheek's faces.

The accountants and auditors requested various files and said they would need the conference room all day. Taylor and Cheek were asked to provide access to bank records and were then excused from the room. I went to Safe Keeping and retrieved the files with Peggy. When I walked by Taylor's office, he and Cheek seemed to be arguing. About fifteen minutes later, I overheard Taylor ask a policeman if he and Cheek could go for lunch at about one o'clock. They were given permission and instructed to return in one hour. As Taylor was leaving the bank, he paused long enough to whisper in my ear, "If I ever find you alone, I'll kill you myself!"

For some reason, I wasn't afraid of Taylor or Cheek. If the embezzlement that we suspected was confirmed, they would be in prison for quite a while, but that didn't rule out that they might put a contract out on me. Or they may be working with Tak. I started to feel that Taylor had hired Jay because when

I noticed his following me, it seemed to coincide with when Julian gave me greater responsibilities at the bank.

I went back to the house and told Julian about the morning events. When I came back to the bank, Taylor and Cheek hadn't returned. At 2:30, the police became concerned and instructed officers to obtain search warrants to enter and search their homes. When the officers returned, they reported that clothes were scattered on the floors, and the houses were in disarray.

Late in the day, the auditors reported all but three sealed collateral envelopes on the Compton loans had blank paper inside. Clive hired a locksmith to change the locks on the doors and the combination to the safe.

That night Julian commented, "All these years, Taylor had a swagger, a bitterness under his breath, but never did I think of him as having a hidden agenda."

Then he looked at me and said, "I will need to replace Taylor, but in the meantime, the current staff can conduct business effectively. Call Clive and instruct him to amend all documents regarding Taylor and Cheek and remove their signatory authority on all accounts and corporate documents.

"I was impressed with Peggy's acumen, capability, and experience. I want to promote her to Head Cashier, assuming Cheek's position, and I want her to handle all my accounts since I cannot sign checks. After you call Clive, get Peggy on the phone, so we can make those changes immediately.

"I need you to spend more time at the bank during this transition period. Virginia will need to find someone to fill in while you're working at the bank until I decide on a replacement for Taylor."

"I can teach my friend Kai the requirements of my position to start with, and I can work with you in the mornings and at the bank in the afternoon. Kai can fill in for me while I'm at the bank, as long as Virginia supervises him."

"Let's get Virginia's approval first, then speak to Kai."

Virginia approved and told me to discuss the opportunity with Kai. I went to see him after work. He lived with Wei Lei's parents in a modest two-bedroom apartment just west of the Seventh Avenue Church. Wei Lei greeted me at the door wearing the white blouse and black slacks that she wore at the cleaners. Her mother wore a white apron and was cooking in a wok, and the smells of onions, garlic, and soy sauce reminded me of Hangzhou. Her father was at the kitchen table and put down the Chinese paper long enough to greet me in Mandarin, which was all her parents spoke.

I asked Wei Lei, "How's your work at Cott's?"

"Not good. I feel like Mrs. Metzger is looking for a reason to fire me."

"What will you do?"

"Clean houses or find a job cooking."

"How's Kai?"

She cast her eyes downward. "He has been stressed at work and wants to quit, but we need the money, especially if I lose my job at Cott's."

"I want Kai to do my job taking care of Mr. LeBlanc during the day. What do you think?"

She hunched her shoulders and shook her head. "He has not been the same since the accident. I hope he will listen to you. He is in the back yard."

As I turned to go outside, she asked, "Will you eat with us?" I nodded.

Kai was sitting on an old crate under a mulberry tree, smoking and littering the ground with butts. An almost empty bottle of whiskey was next to him, and he held a glass in his hand. I sat on another crate near him and looked into his bloodshot eyes.

"Do you want a drink?" he asked, slurring his words.

I shook my head.

"Cigarette?"

When our eyes met, I said, "How long have you been drinking like this?"

He just looked at the ground.

"Is this about the ship launch accident?"

His eyes were listless as he said, "If anything happens to me down at the yard, will you look in on Wei Lei?"

I wondered if he was being threatened at the yard or was still reacting to the launch accident. "There is other work you can do."

"You have become a man of standing and have improved yourself. I can only carry and lift things," Kai slurred.

"I have confidence in you and have a job opportunity to get you out of the yard. I'm spending more time at the bank and need someone to take care of Julian during the week when I'm gone. You can keep your second job at the fish market in the evenings and on weekends. Would you like to work for Julian?"

"I can't do what you do for Mr. LeBlanc," he groaned.

"If you were back in China, you'd take care of your parents. Virginia can train you. You do remember that she sponsored you?"

"I know." He took a deep breath and sighed.

"At Jackson's funeral, you said you needed to get out of the shipyard. The pay will be better, and you'll be treated with respect."

"Wei Lei has been telling me to find something else. Mrs. Metzger has been hassling her, and she's been jittery over losing her job at Cott's. I guess it's time we try something different."

"Good, it's settled."

"Did Wei Lei invite you to dinner?"

"Yes, and it smells wonderful. Let's go eat."

When we stood, Kai took hold of my arm, turned to face me, and we embraced.

Chapter Ten

Late one afternoon, when I returned from the bank, Rhoda said, "Julian wants to see you in his office."

As I entered, a thin Chinese man dressed in a light grey suit with short dark hair and dark brown eyes was sitting in a chair. A shiver ran down my spine as I wondered if Tak sent him.

"Winson, I want to introduce you to Howard Wong. He is a private investigator from China."

I bowed, "Nice to meet you, Mr. Wong," I said in Mandarin. Mr. Wong stood and responded in kind.

"I hired Mr. Wong to locate your family and investigate what happened to them since you left China."

I gasped and couldn't believe what I just heard. "Julian, I'm overwhelmed!"

"Mr. Wong, tell Winson what you know."

"Thank you, Mr. LeBlanc, and nice to meet you, Winson. You probably know it's challenging to obtain information from China. As Mao started seizing control, Chiang Kai-shek fled to Taiwan, and many Chinese citizens with money fled first, while those who remained were told to become Communists, and those who opposed Mao were killed or sent to prison.

"So far, I found no record of your family in Taiwan. Can you tell me what happened that caused you to leave China?"

"Father spoke against Mao, and his supervisor reported him to the authorities, marking our family as objectors. After I left the country, he was to appear at a hearing. Both Mother and Father are educated, Father worked in a factory, and Mother taught science."

"Teachers who taught ideas from the west were purged and taken to the hills to teach the mountain people. It's likely your father was arrested at his hearing and sentenced to a work camp."

I wondered how my family could survive the savagery of Mao's social upheaval. "My sister's name is Lijuan, and she was eleven when I left China. Can you find out if my parents got her out of the country?"

"I need background information on each member of your family. Where you lived, your parent's place of work, birth dates, marriage dates, relatives, any details that might help locate them. Also, information on how you traveled to Canada and who assisted you."

I provided Mr. Wong with the information I could remember and, in doing so, realized my parents may not have expected to see me again, except by a miracle. As YeYe said, my voyage was a flight to safety. Unable to afford transportation, their only hope was finding a Chinese family who would sponsor me. They had no way of knowing the sponsorship opportunity was a front for human trafficking and that Zhang was one of their feeder agents in China.

Suk told me that Dung was a big boss, and now I wondered, was he the head of the snake? Was there a more extensive network? Did Bruno and Jovi, the bosses on the voyage, have a vested interest in seeing us gain access to Canada?

Julian must've seen the concern on my face when he said, "Mr. Wong will try locating your sister and family."

"I can't begin to tell you how much I appreciate this, but if Mr. Wong does indeed find them, then what?"

"The next step would be to connect with a Chinese attorney to see if it will be possible to get them out of the country legally and bring them here," Julian said.

My heart raced. Was it possible I'd see my family again? Should I let myself have hope?

"Winson, did you hear what I said?"

"Yes, Sir. I am…"

"It's okay, take a deep breath. We can't make any promises, but we'll do everything we can to find your family and legally bring them to Canada. Mr. Wong, tell Winson about yourself and how you work."

"I was in the military with Chiang Kai-shek and left on one of the last planes for Taiwan. Many of my family didn't get out and I can't return. I have a friend in an official position in China who privately disapproves of Mao's policies. He does searches for me, and I pay his family in Taiwan. That's the only way he can provide money for them."

"How long will it take to obtain any information?"

"Many people are looking for family members in China, and you aren't my only engagement. I make no promises but will start working with the information you provide. Another issue is that all mail going into and out of China is censored."

"Now, Winson, be patient. That's enough for today, and I need my rest. Call Virginia and Rhoda to help me while you give Mr. Wong any other information you think might help. He will return, but for now, he has his instructions."

Stunned over the magnitude of what Julian wanted to do for me, I was anxious to tell Caitlin, Catherine, and Kai.

I couldn't stop thinking about Mr. Wong's investigation when I came to a difficult realization. How could I tell Kai what Julian was doing for me? Could Mr. Wong have known

Kai's Yeye, who was a Colonel with Chiang Kai-shek? If this search was being done for my parents, but not Kai's, would he be resentful?

I had no money to pay Mr. Wong to look for Kai's parents, and it wasn't my place to talk to Mr. Wong or Julian about Kai. I struggled with not being able to do anything for Kai.

An activity that was so hopeful had become a dilemma.

Chapter Eleven

On a Saturday after breakfast, Julian wanted to go to his office. When he grimaced, I saw pain in his eyes.

"Can I give you some medication?"

"Winson, sit down." He cleared his throat and intently looked at me. "You have done everything I have ever asked of you and without kvetching." He must have seen my puzzlement as he raised his eyebrows, cleared his throat and said, "Without complaining. As you know, I have been contemplating a succession plan for management at the bank. If you're willing, I want to share what I have learned from my years of experience so you can grow and take on more responsibilities. Consider it a mentorship."

Julian was measured in how he conducted his affairs, and I was comfortable with whatever he suggested. "I'm appreciative of any opportunity to learn from you."

"I know you are a quick study, so I want to share a few business and life perspectives.

"Our world is all about building long-term relationships. My father taught me that nothing is more important than a man's honor or 'Shem Tov,' a good name. Reputation is your most valuable asset, and your name reflects your character."

His comment about reputation echoed the principles YeYe taught. They had the same look in their eyes when speaking about life.

"My parent's worldview was cast in their survivor experience. The imprint of the immigrant was never far from the surface. It was their orientation towards life, similar to your own life.

"My father was a man of action, and if not for his conviction to act while in Warsaw, our family may not have survived. He was a realist and told me to keep my eyes wide open, learn what's taking place in the world, and assess the risk and downside of every decision. Ask yourself, what's the expected outcome, and if the worst occurs, can you survive. Do you understand what that means?

"Choose a decision that isn't catastrophic or one you can live with regardless of the outcome."

He started wheezing after each breath, and I asked, "Julian, do you need medication?"

"Yes. We'd better stop. I'm exhausted. Call Virginia, and help me to bed."

∽

A week later, I was rubbing lotion on Julian when he said, "Stop what you're doing and look at me."

"Are you okay?"

"I'm fine, but for the past few days, you have looked perplexed. Is something troubling you?"

I was concerned about how to express my thoughts but decided to come out and say it. "I'm concerned about how people would view doing business at the bank with a Chinese immigrant."

He gave me a puzzled look.

"Customers don't know you're Jewish, and they see you as one of them. Your family changed their name to blend in. Even if I were to change my name, I'd never look like them."

"No doubt. You can't change your skin color or the shape of your eyes, but remember, it's about how you think and who you are inside. I was raised in a society in which most immigrants considered themselves unequal citizens. I didn't consider myself equal to those I was with, and I wasn't. It was agony, but I overcame my feelings. Remember, Canada was built by entrepreneurs who were mostly immigrants."

I wanted to view the world as Julian's father did in Warsaw. As I thought of 'Shem Tov,' I tried to uphold the 'Shem Tov' of my YeYe and began to have a deeper appreciation for the inner strength of my parents and my surrogate parents.

After these talks, I adopted a different perspective. When I walked to the bank, I noticed that everyone wasn't staring at me and that if I smiled at people, some smiled back, but not everyone. Some continued to turn away or spit or mutter under their breath or show some other disapproving gesture.

When I realized that my attitude could make a difference, the wind seemed a little tamer, the waves were less fierce, and the sun not as hot.

Chapter Twelve

Julian gave me additional responsibilities at the bank, and his method of mentoring me was to review bank correspondence together and then dictate an actionable list of items for the day. Mornings were our time together, Julian seemed to enjoy his reengagement, and I cherished the interaction. He told me to take Taylor's office from now on, so customers could see someone in the president's office during business hours.

One day, soon after I arrived at the bank, Peggy knocked at my door and said, "Sir, do you have a few minutes?"

"Good morning Peggy, please come in."

She pulled some statements out of a file folder and spread them on my desk. "Stephanie, in accounting, was reviewing the prior year's income and expense reports. She flagged a series of unidentified expenditures." She pointed at a row of debits.

"Look at these $300 per month checks that were made to a Jason Metzger. The description in the memo line was 'Research.' Do you know who he is and what research was provided?"

"I don't recognize the name. Do you have any information on him?"

"Only a copy of his driver's license that was in the file."

"Let me look at it."

When she handed me the file, I immediately recognized the man in the photo. He had a goatee and grey hair. "I have seen him on the streets of Collingwood. He goes by Jay and has been following me." Then I remembered that Wei

Lei's supervisor at Cott's was named Metzger. Could they be related? When I looked at his driver's license, it indicated he was married.

"What is the address the checks were mailed to?"

"9 Ste. Marie Street."

"That's Cott's Cleaners and is owned by Mrs. Metzger." This confirmed that Taylor hired Jay to follow me. At first, I thought he was working for Mulroney because he was there the day the thugs beat me up, but after his termination from the shipyard, Mulroney could not afford him, and Taylor said he was watching me. Could Jay have worked for both of them?

Peggy interrupted my thoughts, "How do you want me to categorize the expenses?"

"Just put it under spying!"

She looked at me with a puzzled look, then I explained the background and Taylor's remarks. She laughed and said, "I'll mark it under Entertainment Expense. Is there anything else, Sir?"

"Yes, I want you to know you're performing well as Head Cashier, and Mr. LeBlanc is pleased with your work."

"Thank you, Sir. May I say that since you replaced Mr. Taylor, the staff is energized, and they speak to one another more freely and engage in conversation with the customers more often."

"Do you think the staff has a problem with me being Chinese?"

"Sir, they respect your professionalism and appreciate your confidence toward them. People know when they are appreciated."

One Saturday morning, Rhoda brought in the mail and stacked it on his desk for me to sort, open, and read to Julian. There was an envelope from Mr. Wong, postmarked from Taiwan.

It had been over three months since Mr. Wong's visit, and I had put aside thoughts of family because I wanted to avoid false hope and discouragement. It was too emotional for me to consider we might be reunited. Nonetheless, now I was nervous about what I might hear.

When I showed the letter to Julian, he looked at me and said, "Do you want me to read the letter to you, or do you want to read it privately?"

"I want you to read it."

I helped him with his glasses, then set the page on an easel, and he read:

> *Dear Mr. LeBlanc,*
>
> *My man in China found contacts that may help locate Winson's mother and father, but there is no specific information at this time. The Chinese government tells the people outside the republic what Mao thinks they want to hear about China, mostly that all is going well, and his policies are wonderful for the country. They don't disclose that people are not free to speak their minds, sing, listen to music, or even choose what they want to wear. There is only one radio station and one newspaper. The state will arrest people who make unauthorized phone calls or send letters criticizing the government. Any mail received from China is censored. The only way to indicate the real conditions is to use code. My aunt receives letters from her cousin in China. When she sends*

photos of herself, if she's standing, all is well; if sitting,
things are bad. Her latest letter showed her lying down.

Julian stopped and looked at me. I was rubbing my eyes. "My parents and Kai's parents did nothing to deserve being so oppressed."

"Winson, I know." He paused to let me collect my emotions, then asked softly, "Do you want me to continue?"

I nodded.

I am sorry this letter doesn't bring better news, but I hope
we will be able to locate Winson's family. I hope to have
information on his parents in the next few months. I have
found someone willing to deliver Winson's letter if we
find his family. Most likely, all of his prior letters were
destroyed by the censors and never delivered.

I will write again when I hear from my contact.

Sincerely,

Howard Wong

His report increased my anxiety, yet there was nothing I could do.

"Your family loved you and made the same sacrifice my grandparents and parents did for their children. We must trust in the search Mr. Wong is conducting on your behalf. You and I both have our confinements."

"Thank you for all you do for me, it's more than I deserve."

"Now, let's get out of the house! I want to go to the park by the lake for a picnic, and let's take the girls." He surprised me with that suggestion, but my heart lightened, and I broke into a wide grin.

"Yes, Sir. Would it be okay to take Caitlin too?"

"Of course, anytime."

I wanted to be with those I considered family and wished we could include Catherine, Kai, and Wei Lei. Maybe one day, they could all meet my Chinese family.

The lake was beautiful. There were light, billowy clouds, the water was crystal clear, ducks, swans, and geese were squawking and actively searching for food while the pigeons were flapping and cooing. We camped at a picnic table and watched a bicycle caravan of four to six-year-old children chaperoned by two teenage girls, one in front and one in the rear. The little ones had cheery faces and excited voices. As they giggled at each other, their pure joy was infectious. I looked at Caitlin, watching the children with a gleam in her eyes, and was sure she'd want children one day. I thought of how difficult my acceptance in this society had been and didn't want to expose our children to the same prejudice.

Caitlin must've seen concern in my facial expression as she said, "It's okay to be different. You can't predict what's going to happen in any of our lives. It's like standing in the lake and trying to control the current, you must go with the flow."

Thankfully I was distracted by a flock of Canadian geese squawking overhead. I watched them land on the water and then noticed patch of white wildflowers near the shore. I picked a couple, and as I handed them to Caitlin I felt a tug on my shirt from a freckled-faced little girl who had gotten off her bike and was standing in front of me.

She said, "Mister, can I have those flowers?"

Caitlin nodded at me, and I handed them to the little girl. She smiled and put her arms around me in a tight hug. At that moment, I was struck with the thought of having our own child, holding her in my arms, caressing her little head, running my fingers through her hair, and having her rest her head on my shoulder. I would feel so much joy and responsibility as a father. I would make mistakes but would try to teach her like Mother and YeYe taught me, and I would love her with all my heart.

"Bonnie! Bonnie! Stay away from that man," one of the teenage girls snapped as she ran up to us, took the flowers from Bonnie, and pushed them at me. "Don't you go near that…" Little Bonnie turned her head back toward me and was reaching out her hand until the teenager jerked her away.

Like a turtle pulling back into its shell, I started to withdraw when Caitlin took my hand and said, "Honey, the way you looked at Bonnie, I'm sure you have your YeYe's eyes."

"All I know is the way you, Yeye, and Julian look at me is how I want to look at our little ones."

Caitlin pulled my arm and said, "Let's get our feet wet." Her smile softened my heart as she pulled me into the water.

I'd follow her anywhere.

Chapter Thirteen

Julian had hired an investigator to review the old timber inspection reports on file in Ottawa. My next investigative step was to gather additional details of the *Montebello* launch and reconstruct the events before the launch.

I spoke to Kai, but he froze up when Julian or I asked him about the accident. Julian cautioned me about making inquiries because he didn't want to alert management about our investigation, so I couldn't talk to current shipyard employees. I needed to find men who were under the ship, saw what went wrong, and were no longer employed. Since management didn't offer disability or retirement benefits, former employees may not have company loyalties and might be receptive to my questions.

The Coffey sisters or Mildred were close to Jackson and might know who he worked with on the launch crew. Entering the Seventh Avenue Church always gave me warm feelings. Ruth was preparing a meal, and when she saw me, she washed her hands and greeted me with a big hug.

"Do you want tea and a slice of homemade apple pie?"

I smiled and eagerly said yes.

She steeped tea, cut the pie, then sat by ourselves when she asked, "What happened between you and Caitlin's father?"

I told her about my encounter with YeYe because she'd understand. She squeezed my arm and conveyed recognition with her eyes and a nod.

"I told Caitlin I'd investigate what happened before the launch to see if we could find answers for the causes of the accident. I wish I could speak to Jackson, he would've known what happened or who to talk to. Did he ever say anything to you or Miriam about the launch in the weeks before the accident?"

"We saw Jackson less and less because he was working long hours, but he often spoke about two men he worked with on different assignments."

"Do you remember their names?"

"One was named Jeep. I don't know his last name. The other was George, with an unusual last name. Let me think, it sounded like arb, or ar-bor. Wait, it was Arbott, George Arbott."

"Do you know if they live in Collingwood?"

"I can ask Frank, he delivers the mail to almost everybody in town."

"This is important, please ask Frank if he knows them and if they still work at the yard. I can't talk to anyone who is still employed there."

"I think Jeep's retired, but I will ask Frank about George."

I thanked Ruth and told her I needed a break in my investigation and it might come through one of them.

During dinner, I told Caitlin about Jeep and George.

"I know that Jeep's daughter has taken piano lessons from Catherine. His last name is Cooper. I will ask Catherine if she can arrange a meeting with him."

"That's terrific. I can't trust anyone who still works in the yard, so be sure and ask if he still works there. I will let Ruth know she only needs to find George."

She got tears in her eyes as she looked at me and said, "I love you and am grateful that you're trying to help my parents. This means more to me than words can express."

"I haven't solved any problems yet, but we've taken some positive steps."

Two days later, Caitlin was excited as she greeted me after work. "Catherine said Jeep is retired, and she arranged for you to meet him. He knows it's about *Montebello* and wants you to come to his house at 421 Minnesota Street at 8:00 p.m. on Wednesday."

Minnesota Street was where many ship captains had their homes. Many of these houses were grand, made of stone, three stories with a basement, large wrap-around porches, and beautifully landscaped yards.

Jeep's house was at the end of the street, farthest away from the harbor. At this end of the block, the homes were one story, with basements, and occupied by working-class families.

When I walked up, a large man in blue overalls was puttering around in the garage. He turned, looked at his watch, and said in a loud, boisterous voice, "You must be Winson. Catherine said you were coming. Glad you're on time. Come in."

He spoke with a heavy accent, his face was reddish and looked swollen, he was broad-shouldered and tall, with big hands and thick arms, and his large frame supported an extended belly. We walked in through the parlor and went into the kitchen, where the smell of freshly baked cookies filled the air.

"Betty, this is Winson." She wore a yellow and brown plaid dress and had black shoulder-length hair.

"Nice to meet you, Winson. Catherine spoke highly of you. Would you like tea and cookies?"

"Yes ma'am, thank you. It smells wonderful in here."

"I just took the cookies out of the oven. I'll make a kettle of tea."

We sat at the kitchen table and Jeep filled the chair, and seemed as big sitting as he was standing.

"I understand you're retired," I said.

He looked at me funny, then said, "Come again? You have to speak louder, too many years in the yard where there was always loud noises."

I raised my voice. "Are you retired?"

"Oh, no. I work for the little lady around the house all day." He laughed as he looked in Betty's direction, and she smiled at him. "I planned to retire from the yard in another year or two, but the accident did me in, and I never went back. Now, you have questions for me?"

"Yes, Sir, and thank you for seeing me."

"Ask."

"The *Montebello* launch, what went wrong?"

"What went wrong? That's the question, isn't it? What do you know?"

"I worked in the shipyard several years ago, building the support structure. During the morning of the launch, I was in the yard."

"You were there! Were you working?"

"No, I was watching the men underneath the ship from the edge of the basin, just inside the gate. Something seemed out of place, and when I heard *Montebello* groaning, well, you know what happened."

"You were there, huh."

I nodded as he seemed to stare straight through me. I said, "I read several investigative reports which targeted Kierian Mulroney as the cause, saying he gave the launch signal early. But I watched him that day, and he never gave the signal."

"Ah, yes."

He had several newspaper articles on the table, he lifted one to me. "Look here, some blamed it on the triggers. They hold the ship in place. The tighter the triggers are, the better they hold until the ropes are cut away and the ship is released. They say in this article, they broke at the last moment.

"You know *Montebello* had three engines which weighed 350 tons each, larger than any other ship we ever built. It was a lot of weight. When they drove the wedges, it didn't lift the ship like previous launches. They had to bring in jacks, three hundred-ton jacks, to help with the weight. About thirty to forty minutes before the launch, they drive out the wedges, from one end of the ship to the other. Well, I was alongside the ship when they started to drive them out, and my supervisor was concerned about the extra weight and says to me, we better get on board and get out from under her. We climbed toward the top, and he yells, 'get moving,' because he could see something happening on the end.

"He saw the ship move before it was supposed to. There were hundreds of guys underneath. This was bad for them because they had no way out. Just after we stepped on her deck, the whistles started blowing, and we could feel the ship move, meaning something went wrong, very wrong!"

He started coughing and puffing, then he took a swallow of water and paused to catch his breath. His expression and body language changed as if he was reliving the experience. "I was hanging on to the railing for dear life. Everybody started running to get out of the way. Men climbed or stepped over other men and were ducking boards that were flipping every which way. Well, you saw it.

"We were lucky to make it to the top before things went wrong because when she moved, there was massive water displacement. It swept men into the backwash, thrust them into the wall then back against the ship. Thirty feet of water went over the wall then came back in like a tidal wave. No one was supposed to be under the ship when she launched." His eyes widened as he wiped his mouth with the back of his hand.

"The drag chains were violently pulled in one direction, then back the other way with the water coming back. Those chains cut men into pieces. You saw the boxes, twenty-five with anchor chains, them chains sweeping back and forth with the surf. Men were caught in between and couldn't get out, so they started to crawl up ropes trying to survive."

Chills went up my spine, and I started breathing hard. We were both reliving a traumatic event.

I said, "When the whistles blew, I ran toward the ship and saw men running in the opposite direction with sledgehammers frozen in their hands. My friend, Kai, was driving wedges that morning and said a man walked over his back, and someone pulled him up just before a drag chain fell and split the sandbag pile he had been laying on."

"Everyone was trying to help. Let me show you pictures." He pulled out a box of photos. "Look here at all these heavy boxes and chains. In this picture are the 350-ton engines. *Montebello* was too heavy and too long."

"Was that one possible cause for the failure?"

"You need to speak louder." He pointed to his ears, and I repeated my question.

Jeep said, "My friends tell me they don't plan to use wood beams underneath the ship anymore. They're switching to steel, so they must've found problems. Since you worked there, you know they reused wooden triggers year after year on launches. Many had cracked, and they could have caused the hull to break loose prematurely. Inspectors certified they were safe to use, but we had our suspicions about their condition."

"I worked on building the ship's platform, but I know the triggers lift the ship for the launch. I thought they used new timbers on every ship."

Betty interrupted, and as she served tea and cookies, Jeep said to her, "Betty, bring us whiskey."

"Didn't you want tea?"

"I said to bring us whiskey, Woman!" He gave her a stern look, and she meekly withdrew.

"Now, where were we? Oh yeah. I think there is a good chance the engine's extra weight and problems with the trigger boards led to the ship's premature movement." He took a deep breath and asked, "Did you know that Simco was acquired a couple of years ago by a big corporation? Business was down, and they didn't have another order for a ship, so they cut expenses and laid off men months before the launch."

Betty brought two shot glasses of whiskey. Jeep downed his shot and said, "Woman, bring us another round."

Listening to Jeep brought back the horrors from that day. I hadn't taken a drink since I went to work for Julian, and I was stressed by remembering what I saw and experienced that morning in the yard. Besides, I wanted to maintain a rapport with Jeep, so I closed my eyes and took the shot. It was like a bolt of lightning to my system. "Wow!" I said as I shook my head.

Betty poured us two more shots.

She looked at Jeep, then me.

I pushed my shot toward Jeep, then he looked at me and said, "From the look on your face, you don't drink, do you?"

"No, Sir."

He laughed as he banged on the table and said, "Take another shot."

This second one went down smoother, but my head was fuzzy. "I think I'll take that tea now," I said.

"No wonder you stopped working at the yard," Jeep chuckled.

He downed his shot, then looked at Betty for another round.

"Do you know which agencies investigated the accident?" I asked.

"The government, labor unions, insurance men, when people get killed or hurt, they all investigate."

"There were lawsuits."

"How do you know about the lawsuits?"

"I went to the City offices to look at the files and reports. I was told the files were all sealed due to the lawsuits."

"I have my suspicions."

Betty put the almost empty bottle on the table and gave him a look. He poured another shot, downed it, and reflected, "The unions were cross with the owners. There were issues with wages, workmen's compensation, and working conditions. We didn't want to lose our jobs, so when the managers told us to keep quiet or else, we did."

As he stared off into the distance, I could see the muscles in his jaw flexing, his hands clenched, and he shuffled his feet back and forth. It seemed as if he were about to explode. Finally, he stopped moving for several minutes. I thought he was about to say something when he let out a groan, and his eyes glistened. He choked out, "I saw men and body parts floating in the water. I knew most of those men and worked with them for years."

He poured the rest of the whiskey into his glass and gulped it!

"Every day, I still think about what happened. I forget the other launches, but I don't forget that one. I bet you don't either. Woman, bring me another bottle."

"Jeep, you've had enough," Betty said.

"Woman, another bottle, now!" He banged hard on the table, then started coughing and tried catching his breath.

"It's difficult when I think about the tragedy of that day. I appreciate what you have shared with me." When his eyes lost their focus, I felt it was time for me to go.

Jeep said, "I relive those events every day. I never want to see another ship launch."

When I returned home, I told Caitlin the details of my visit with Jeep. She could see I was shaken and kept hugging me. When I settled down, she said, "I have news too. Ruth called and spoke with George Arbott's wife. She said George left the yard after the accident and never returned. He sent his wife to pick up his final paycheck, and they're in a financial pinch because he has worked sparingly since the accident.. Ruth offered to pay George if he'd be willing to talk about the accident and arranged through Mrs. Arbott to meet with you Sunday morning."

"They don't go to church?"

"Ruth said they haven't gone since the accident. She said not to expect much, but just see what George is willing to tell you."

It was a cold, damp day when I went to meet George. His wife greeted me at the door. "Good morning Mr. Winson. My name is Anna, Anna Arbott."

She was small and thin, her brown hair was pulled back, and she wore a caramel-colored dress. I stood outside as she patted down her hair as if embarrassed by her appearance.

"Times have been tough for us. George hasn't spoken to anyone about the accident since he left the yard on the day of the launch. I'm a seamstress and do any work I can find to keep the household together. You see, George drinks most days and can't get himself together to find work. Your money is appreciated."

She paused to study my face.

"Thank you for allowing me to speak to your husband."

"I understand you're working to find out what caused the accident."

"Yes, and I need to speak to men who were at the launch but no longer work at the shipyard."

"Please wait here for a minute while I let George know you're here."

She went back into the house. Amid the sound of loud, argumentative voices, there was a loud thud.

When Mrs. Arbott opened the screen door, she said, "George will see you now. But please, give him time. He's hesitant to open up." She spoke with a shaky voice without making eye contact.

I was cautious as I walked into the house and expected the unexpected. The room was dark, and there was a chill in the air with only embers smoldering in the fireplace. George was sitting in an overstuffed chair with worn arms, dressed in jeans and a grey flannel shirt with two pockets. He was gaunt and had a scruffy beard.

Without looking at me, he said, "What's it you want to talk about?"

Anna glared at George and then said to me, "Winson, please take a seat."

The interaction between them was like two cats circling before a fight.

"I'd like to discuss the weeks before the *Montebello* accident and the day of the launch."

"There isn't anything to talk about." He took a drink from a dirty glass. Whiskey was heavy on his breath. I didn't know what to say, so I looked at Anna.

"George, we took the money! All he wants is to talk about the launch."

"I haven't a thing to say."

"George. George! Now you're going to talk to this young man."

"I got nothin to say to him."

I started to rise. Anna put her hand on my shoulder and gave a light downward press.

"Now, George," her tone was unrelenting. "You're going to talk to him because I do everything to keep this house together, and all you do is drink your days away. I'm not going to let you crawl back into your bottle. We need this money! Now talk to this man and answer all his questions."

George looked away, "I can't."

"George, we have an agreement with this young man."

"Take your money, leave! It's the devil's bargain."

"The devil loves unspoken secrets. Especially those which fester in a man's soul," I replied.

He sighed and his shoulders released.

"Years ago, I worked in the yard and was there the morning of the launch," I added.

George looked me in the eyes for the first time. His face was devoid of expression.

"You were there?"

"Yes. I heard *Montebello* groan before she went. Then I helped pull men out of the water. It was a disaster."

He stared at me with a blank expression on his face.

"Okay, young man, you ask George your questions," Anna commanded as George looked up. She was feisty and needed to be.

"May I bring you tea?" Anna asked.

"Yes, please."

I turned towards George, "I talked with Jeep about the accident a few days ago."

"You talked with Jeep?"

"Yes."

"I haven't seen him since the day of the accident." His stern expression relaxed a bit.

"I'm trying to learn what went wrong with the launch. Can you tell me what you saw?"

"You spoke to Jeep?" George repeated as he fingered his almost empty glass.

"He shared his experiences with me on the day of the launch."

George stared towards a picture on the wall. "I shouldn't have been underneath that ship. It was usually welders, shipwrights, and erectors. They had to have extra people because of the extra weight and size of the ship. What did Jeep say?"

"He said the engines were heavier than anything previously installed."

Anna's dimples showed as she smiled while serving tea.

"Thank you, Ma'am," I took a sip.

"Those were 10,000 horsepower Selzer diesel engines. Roy Neal and I assembled them. Engines are usually installed after the launch, but our cranes couldn't lift so much weight that far out, so they were installed before the launch. They had to ballast the side tanks forward with an equal weight of water to compensate for the extra weight on the stern, to hopefully make her come down the launchways even. The ship had to travel about eighty feet. She was seventy-five feet wide and about four feet from the edge of the dock."

As he started to talk, he began to relax. I could see the tension start to leave his body, and he began to speak in a calmer voice.

"This was why we needed extra crew on launch day and why I was underneath the ship. Pipefitters, electricians, many workers who wouldn't normally have been underneath all were there, about 300 of us." He had calmed down and spoke in a monotone about the engines.

"Then there were the television crews. They wanted to keep the launch on schedule for high noon, and the company dignitaries were making a fuss about being on time. The extra weight took us longer to drive the wedges, so there was a bit of a rush, which is never good with a complex launch."

"Where were you when the ship started to move?"

He swallowed hard, and his eyes glazed.

"I was near the bow, not on the waterside, but the dockside. A crane was parked right next to me. The day before, Horace Swartz and I wandered around the deck and talked to Paul

Williamson, a shipmate, who told us he was terrified of what was happening underneath the ship. He said she had already settled six inches, and she'd been groaning for several days as if something was starting to give way."

"Could it mean the wood was giving way the day before the launch?" I asked.

"Something was giving way, the wood, the earth underneath, the extra weight, or a combination of factors. As Paul said, something was happening underneath. He told me it wasn't safe and that we needed to talk to somebody about it. I told Horace I would make gall darn sure I was out toward the end, so if anything went wrong, I was outta there. I wasn't going to be far under the ship the next day, even if I was fired. I didn't realize I was going to be in front of one of those anchor boxes that drags forward when the ship launches, but I beat it! I beat it!" His voice rose as if he were in front of the ship once again.

"I was running, carrying my sledgehammer! I didn't even think to drop it. I carried it all the way home," he shouted.

Then he leaned forward with a fierce look and stared at an invisible object in midair.

After a minute, he melted back in his chair.

Anna's eyes enlarged as she said, "The night before the launch, I told George if I heard the whistles blow at the wrong time, I'd go bananas because I knew he was working underneath. I was terrified that he'd be killed. So when the whistles blew before noon, I went crazy. I ran to the docks, and everyone was in a frenzy. Sirens and whistles were blowing, people on loudspeakers yelling directions, ambulances going back and forth. I grabbed whoever was near me and shouted George's name to them, and asked if they knew where he was.

When they couldn't or wouldn't answer, I grabbed someone else. I wasn't the only wife doing this.

"Mister, you can't imagine what I went through until I found George at home. It was me that had to pry that damn hammer from his hands. He just wouldn't let go."

She stopped and looked at George for a moment, then continued, "He was in shock. I wanted to take him to the hospital, but he wouldn't hear of it."

"I was searching too. My friend Jackson and my boss's son Joseph didn't make it. My friend Kai escaped, but he's still in shock."

After a few moments of silence, George said, "Most people worked there because it's the best paying job in town, nobody paid anything close to shipyard wages. There was a demand for welders, burners, pipefitters, plumbers, electricians, and finishing trades. I was twenty-two when I started there.

"There was a new company that opened near Owen Sound. They had more advanced methods of building and launching ships and could do it better and cheaper. Our shipyard started laying off people before the accident happened. Did Jeep say there were a lot of layoffs?"

"Yes, and he said there were problems with the timbers used for the triggers. Many were used more than once."

George bolted out of his chair and started pacing back and forth.

I looked at Anna, and she appeared to be as startled as I was. George raised his voice and said, "Those sons of bitches! I couldn't believe the condition of some of the lumber. There was a lot of shit going on."

Anna said, "George, it's over. It was a long time ago. Calm down."

"Bloody hell! You don't know what it was like that day. Nobody does that wasn't there. It was like a mountain falling on you with no way to escape. I need whiskey."

Anna rose and quickly brought us shots.

George wrapped his long thin hand around the glass, downed it, and then looked at her for another. Anna watched me.

I drank with Jeep and felt it would make George more comfortable, so I took the shot. When George yelled for more whiskey, Anna was hesitant but headed back to the kitchen.

She returned with another shot for each of us. As I drank mine, I relaxed and remembered how opium and cigarettes helped me deal with the stress of working in the ship's boiler room on the voyage from China, and I knew that it could settled George's nerves.

He settled back into his chair and muttered, "Montebello was the fourth accident in the past few years. It's what convinced me to leave the yard. Jeep probably told you about the previous accident when the top of a crane collapsed and a sixty-five-ton section fell. We both almost drowned."

He paused like he had a dry mouth. Anna put another shot in front of him. He downed it quickly, wiped his mouth, gave her a hard stare, and said, "Another."

He stared at her until she got up.

"The next accident was another crane falling. I was working in the engine room and had to go to the machine shop. The crane was lifting a screen bulkhead, so the welders could work on the other side of it, and the boom collapsed and split the building that housed the welding shop in half. Guys were bailing out of the shop like rats. Several people were hurt.

"After these accidents, I was serious about leaving. The day the launch went bad, I knew I was on borrowed time." He jumped up and kicked the footstool across the room and paced again like a caged tiger.

Anna brought a glass of water and placed it on the table next to the tea. He squinted his eyes at her.

"George, you know what we have talked about," she said.

He looked at the water, paused, picked up the cup of tea, took a sip, then spit it onto the floor. Anna looked at me, and I nodded.

With a harsh voice, she said to George, "I'll get you one more shot."

Then he continued pacing while describing the morning of the launch. "The ship lurched out, dragging the boxes chained to stop its movement, then when it swung back toward the dock, it created huge waves in that small basin. All those displaced timbers heaved up and down, back and forth, the men trapped in the water were crushed by huge beams. They had nowhere to go."

George stopped talking for a minute, then said, "I'll never forget the screaming. I saw one guy crushed by a block of wood the size of a car."

He looked at me and asked, "Where was Jeep?"

"On the top of the ship. He saw body parts floating in the water after the ship settled, so did I."

"I never talked about it and never told anyone what I saw, including Anna." He looked at her as she brought him a shot, which he downed immediately. "I can't forget seeing the floating guts and arms and legs and heads and…"

At this point, he just stopped talking. His face looked as if he saw these things again right there in front of him.

Finally, he began again, "A few days after the accident, I got a call from one of the managers and gave an account of what I saw. But I never saw it in any of the written reports. This is the first time I heard of other eyewitnesses seeing the same thing."

He fingered the empty glass and looked at Anna, he wanted another shot, and she shook her head.

"Do you think there was pressure from the shipyard management to keep the accidents and other issues from the investigative authorities?" I asked.

"Sure there was. When the manager called me, he said if I wanted to keep my job, I'd keep quiet about what happened in the yard. I didn't want to jeopardize my friends' jobs or bring trouble to me even though I didn't intend to go back.

"Shipyards are a dangerous place. You're working on slippery steel, tons of steel lifted above you, there are always accidents when working with heavy equipment. Work doesn't stop even in inclement weather, and we operated during the worst of the winter storms. You know! You worked there."

I looked at my hands and rubbed the ring and little finger on my left hand, which often ached from working in freezing weather for long periods.

He awkwardly sat down and looked at the floor as he said, "Do you have any other questions?"

I could tell it was time to end the conversation. "Thank you for your time. I know it was hard for you, as it is for me, to relive that day." I had a lump in my throat.

When I handed him the money, he pushed it back toward me and said, "Here, take your money." He stared in the distance, then looked at me and said, "It was good for me to talk."

Anna spoke up, "Now you two have gotten too carried away. I made the arrangement and will be keeping the money. You hear me, George Arbott?"

"George, keep the money," I said.

"Young man, what you told me about what Jeep shared was the first time another person said they saw what I did."

Anna hugged George and kissed him on the cheek.

"I can't escape the memories I have from that day," George said as he looked at me and offered his hand. I took it.

Anna walked me to the door and said, "Just getting him to talk about it may be a turning point. He's a good man, but he hasn't been the same since the accident."

"Thank you for making this meeting possible. I wish the best for you both."

That night I tossed and turned and had vivid dreams.

I heard Caitlin's soft voice and felt her gentle hand on my arm, "Winson, wake up! What are you dreaming about? You were thrashing and making an awful sound like you were trying to scream?"

"I was in freezing water, and there was a ceiling of logs that blocked out the sun. I tried moving my arms and legs, but they felt heavy, and the water was like a thick gel that kept me suspended. Then I saw bodies off in the distance, moving in my direction. I was frozen, but I could feel the current taking them past me. Bodies with desperate stares streamed by like a school of fish and reached out to torment me. Detached arms and legs came at me, my arms wouldn't move, and I tried kicking my legs, but I couldn't push them away, and they started to hit against me.

"A body came up from below, and I was face to face with Fukan, a Korean boy on the voyage to Canada, who drowned during a storm trying to release a barge with me. His big eyes kept staring at me. I felt myself screaming, but I couldn't make a sound." Perspiration rolled down my neck.

"You were having a nightmare and started yelling for help, and that's when I woke you. Let's get you washed up and changed. All this stress is playing out in your subconscious."

Chapter Fourteen

It was a crisp fall morning, so after breakfast, a massage, and a sponge bath, I took Julian out on the porch for fresh air. "Julian, I want to discuss the *Montebello* accident and what we have discovered."

"Help me get comfortable. I want the warmth on my neck, turn my back to the sun, then tell me what you know."

I positioned him and then said, "I spoke to two men who worked at the shipyard on launch day. George Arbott was positioned under the ship. Jeep Cooper was on the top deck. They each shared what the circumstances were at the shipyard before and after the accident from their perspective."

I recounted the conversations with Jeep and George for Julian and summarized the events leading up to the catastrophe.

"Excellent research, you have become a good investigator. I made some inquiries, too, and discovered several relevant items. First, the company wanted to expand the shipyard. It petitioned the government several years ago for additional land that could be dredged to lengthen the pier for the dry dock and launch structure. The request was approved, and the dock where this ship was built was lengthened. My sources indicated that the soil may not have been properly engineered or compacted correctly because there was settling. With this ship's size and extra weight, the extended dock may have contributed to the premature movement.

"Clive researched the shipyard ownership and discovered that the controlling interest of the company was purchased two years ago by Peabody-McCall Enterprises, a diversified conglomerate with a subsidiary that performs testing, inspections, and certifications. The CEO of Peabody-McCall was a former finance minister in the federal government and, this is only an assumption, but his influence may have induced the government to facilitate extending the dock into the bay. If the testing unit used for inspections was a subsidiary of Peabody-McCall, it could be a conflict of interest."

I was wide-eyed and surprised at Julian's disclosures.

He smiled and said, "I will have Clive consult with a friend in Ottawa regarding this new evidence and our theories, then see what it would take to reopen the accident investigation. Given the influence and broad interests of the new ownership, it will need to be an airtight case for the government to reconsider, and even then, it will be difficult to prove conclusively. Would the two men you interviewed provide testimony?"

"I'm sure Jeep would. George might be hesitant, but if Jeep cooperates, that may convince George. They both indicated they were suspicious."

Julian said, "I think we may be able to prove that certifications of the launch timbers were falsified. A source said the certifying inspector was charged with two counts of driving while intoxicated since the accident. If he knew his certifications indirectly caused deaths and injuries, drinking might be his narcotic, like it was for Joseph."

Julian choked up when he mentioned Joseph. He cleared his throat and then continued, "But, if the testing company was owned by Peabody-McCall, they will contest any allegations.

"Here's our strategy. We'll have my source contact the inspector who certified the report, present the evidence we've obtained from eyewitnesses and tell him we're going to reopen the case through the federal government in Ottawa. If we can scare him into wanting a plea bargain for immunity, he may disclose information. It would be helpful if he has deposit tickets for any money he was paid by the shipbuilding company. The most crucial evidence to obtain would be a statement under oath that much of the wood used on this launch was below code specifications.

"We need to work with people I know in the Royal Canadian Mounted Police crime unit. If the inspector cooperates, his testimony to participate in the commission hearing would be essential to consider probable charges being filed against the company."

Julian was dry-mouthed, so I poured him water and held the straw up to his lips. More water than usual dribbled down his chin as I held up a napkin and gave him more to drink.

Then he continued, "You know that Simco and its parent company will do whatever it takes to repudiate any allegations and may come after us as a defensive maneuver. It could also get unpleasant because it impacts the entire community."

He looked into my eyes with rapt attention, "What do you think?"

I paused, thinking about how this could adversely affect Julian and the bank, then said, "We should do what's right. This is important to a lot of people in the community."

"I was hoping you would say that. Let's see how far this takes us."

Chapter Fifteen

1964

Three months later, on a Monday afternoon, I was in my office at the bank when there was a knock at my door. A well-dressed man wearing leather gloves and holding a fedora was standing in the doorway.

"Excuse me, I'm Detective Inspector Albert Picard with the Ontario Provincial Police." His tone was clipped and matched his crisp-knotted skinny tie. His dark blue suit perfectly set off his light complexion, and the only thing that marred his appearance was his thick-rimmed glasses.

"I'm overseeing the bank embezzlement case with the local police department. I'm here to report what we discovered regarding Compton, Taylor, and Cheek."

I stood, shook his hand, then ushered him into my office. "Pleased to meet you, Inspector. May I offer you coffee or tea?"

"Thank you. Coffee with sugar."

After he was served coffee, he measured spoons full of sugar, and I watched him count the number of stirs under his breath before taking a small sip. I thought he may as well drink maple syrup.

"We have concluded our investigation of the bond certificates collateralizing the bank loans to Compton. The bank examiner was interviewed and eventually admitted that he knew Taylor wasn't providing all the collateral certificates for the annual review. The loans he reviewed did contain bond certificates. As you know, the other loans had blank paper inside the collateral envelopes.

"Do you know why he did it?"

"He admitted to receiving $500 after each examination for the last five years. After lunch at the country club, Taylor would hand him an envelope with cash."

"What's the status of the examiner?"

"He's been terminated for breach of duty. The Office of the Inspector General of Banks will determine how he's to be charged, including if he's to be included as an accomplice."

At least partial justice was administered.

"Do you know the history between Compton and Taylor?" I asked.

"Years ago, Roger Compton and Oliver Taylor were members at the same country club in Toronto and played golf and gambled together. Compton was delinquent on his provincial taxes, in need of cash, and took money intended for investment in Adolph's plant and equipment to support his personal expenses. When Compton's father died, he inherited a portfolio of corporate bonds. Taylor seized on an opportunity to receive compensation from Compton by approving his loan requests with bond certificates as collateral.

"Taylor would present additional bond certificates as collateral for subsequent loans and, within the first week after each loan was funded, he deposited a check from Compton to a credit union account for himself. Taylor transferred a percent of the funds to another credit union account to compensate Cheek, who was part of the scheme. A repeated pattern of these loans, transfers, and deposits occurred over five years.

"The collateral backing all but three of the loans was counterfeit, and those loans have defaulted. Our investigation indicated that the losses sustained by the bank totaled $286,185. Compton and Taylor intentionally misappropriated loan proceeds without the consent or knowledge of Merchants Bank and Trust Board or Julian LeBlanc. Under Canadian law, we have filed charges of embezzlement and conspiracy to commit bank fraud against Taylor, Cheek, and Compton. We ordered the seizure of assets in their bank accounts. That being said, all the assets from Taylor and Cheek's accounts have been withdrawn. There was $3,458 in Compton's account."

He paused as I was taking notes, when I looked up, he continued.

"We arrested Compton in Toronto, and he is currently out on bond. We issued warrants for Taylor and Cheek. We searched throughout Ontario and adjoining provinces, without success, and suspect they have fled to the United States. We filed extradition requests, and the U.S. is cooperating with our department, but they have been unable to locate Taylor or Cheek."

"Do you think they will be found?"

"It's highly unlikely given the circumstances. We're limited as to what we can do with our corresponding agency in America. We'll keep our investigation open, and if there is any new information, you will be contacted."

After Picard left, I gazed out the window and thought how unfortunate that Taylor and Cheek weren't arrested the first day when the Police entered the bank.

Chapter Sixteen

Weeks later, I pushed Julian into his office, situated him behind his desk, and started to go through the day's mail when I saw a letter from Mr. Wong on the top of the mail stack.

When I showed it to Julian, he said, "Ask Rhoda to prepare two cups of tea and let's read this letter together."

I was shaking and didn't call Rhoda. Instead, I put the kettle on and stood in a daze waiting for the water to boil.

Virginia entered the kitchen as I stood with my head down, rubbing my fingers. She asked, "What's wrong, eh?"

"We received a second letter from Mr. Wong today, and Julian is going to read it to me."

"You're squeezing your hands."

I pushed my hands in my pockets but couldn't stop shifting my weight from one foot to the other.

"I care for you. Would you let me sit in and listen?"

"I'd appreciate your being with me. I want Caitlin here too, but she's teaching today, and I'm too anxious to wait until she comes home."

We went into Julian's office together. Julian looked up. "I see you have enlisted Virginia for support."

I managed a smile.

"Winson, I want you to sit down. Virginia will help me with the easel. We'll read the letter together."

He watched me sit as Virginia set the first page on the easel and said, "Are you ready?"

"Ready as I'll ever be."

Dear Mr. LeBlanc,

My informant, Mr. Pai, went to Winson's former home. Several families lived there who knew nothing of Winson's family, but they showed him an old, tattered journal with many missing pages. It was dated 1949, so Pai paid money for it because it could have been written by Winson's mother. He could not get the entire journal out of the country, so he sent some legible pages with pertinent information, which are enclosed with this letter. He will try to send the remaining pages a little at a time.

"Virginia, give Winson the journal pages."

Virginia handed me two tattered pages, yellowed and dog eared.

My hands were trembling as I looked at the first page. "Oh! This is mother's careful writing of Chinese characters." I clutched them to my chest.

"Do you want me to continue, or do you want to read them now?" Julian asked.

"Please continue. I haven't read Chinese for a long time. It'll take me a few minutes to translate."

Julian continued:

As Pai was leaving, one of the older boys stopped him and admitted to being in Winson's mother's class. Pai asked if he knew what had happened to her. He said a student from her class joined the Communist Party and believed Mao was the people's savior. When Mao started pushing a vast campaign to purify the country, this student reported her to the authorities.

Soldiers entered her classroom, seized her in front of her students and accused her of promoting western ideas, ridiculed her, cut her long hair in front of the class, burned her books, and then took her into custody to appear before the district council. The student was proud of what he had done because he told the class that he had turned her in. The boy told Pai that your mother was his favorite teacher and missed her. He did not know he was living in her house.

We know many teachers were sent into the mountains to teach peasants and were never allowed to return to the city.

I gasped as I struggled for composure.
"Take a minute to calm yourself," Virginia said.
I took a few sips of tea, and Julian continued:

At this time, we know nothing of her whereabouts. We do have some contacts in the mountain communities and hope to get a lead on her.

Winson's father was prosecuted for his public comments about Mao and was beaten in front of the courthouse and transferred to an unidentified work camp. Lijuan was taken into the service of a district warlord.

I'm sorry this letter is not very encouraging, but I still hope to find Winson's parents. It will be more challenging to find Lijuan. When I have additional information, I will write again.

Sincerely,

Howard Wong

I must have been gritting my teeth because my jaw was sore. My little sister was a concubine. If it was possible to trade places with her or mother, I would.

"He didn't say anything about my grandfather."

"No, but remember, it takes time because information must be acquired without the knowledge of the communist authorities. Do you want to read the journal pages privately?"

I did not think I could hold the pages steady, so I closed my eyes and felt drawn into another world. I don't know how long I sat there, unable to move or speak, when I heard Julian's voice, "Winson, Winson," and opened my eyes.

I took a deep breath and said, "I want you both to hear my mother's words, so you have a sense of her. I may stumble on some of the translations."

I lifted one of the tattered pages and turned it until the date was at the top. I studied the writing and found I remembered more than I expected as I slowly translated out loud:

December 17, 1949

> *I watched my son board a ship for Canada today, answering to a new name, going to a place where he knows no one and doesn't speak the language. Did we make the right decision?*

I put the page down and paused as my eyes became fluid. I didn't care if tears ran down my cheeks.

As I touched Mother's journal pages and saw her beautiful calligraphy, I pictured her wearing her favorite blue floral-print silk dress and smelled her lavender perfume. I imagined her gentle hand pushing my hair to one side, away from my eyes, and her voice reading softly to me. I took a deep breath and continued:

I miss him so much.

I choked out the words. Virginia sat down next to me and patted my knee. I took a sip of tea and hadn't realized how dry my mouth had become. Then I continued:

Yang's Bookstore was closed by the army, all his books were burned, and he is in prison. At school, teachers are concerned about Mao threatening anyone who deviates from his doctrines. Out of concern for Lijuan and Father, I may need to change my opinions if we are to survive. I don't know what would happen if I lost my job?

The house is empty without Wen Shun. I see his face everywhere I look. I hope we will receive a letter from him soon. Agent Zhang told me it will be several days before the ship makes the first port. I will take our letters to Zhang, hoping he will send them to one of the ports.

I started smoking, and Lijuan asked me to stop. I know Tai is worried about his hearing because he does not want to talk and is drinking too much. Father spends most of the day in his workshop. We are all feeling sad and overwhelmed. I cannot imagine what Wen Shun is feeling.

We hope to remain cloistered from what's happening with Mao and pray to live a peaceful life; however, I fear that is impossible.

When I read her entry about living a peaceful life, I shook. Virginia put her arm around my shoulder and handed me her handkerchief.

"Winson, take a few moments. There's no rush."

I appreciated Julian's kind words. There was one more page, and I read the first words silently, then paused, looked up at Julian and Virginia, took several deep breaths, and read:

January 24, 1950

> *Tai had his hearing before the council and was sentenced to seven years in a work camp, then publicly humiliated and beaten. I do not know where he was sent or if we will ever be together again.*

> *I agonize over the choice I made to send Wen Shun to Canada. We wanted to give him an opportunity for freedom. Tai took the blame so Wen Shun wouldn't be angry at me. He said it was the least he could do to make up for not knowing how to love his son.*

> *Tai had a difficult life, losing his mother when he was young and being traumatized by fighting in the war against Japan. My husband knew he was too hard on Wen Shun, so to protect him, I made an arrangement with Tai to let me discipline and raise him.*

I stopped reading, put the page down, looked away, then said, "I was in the same house with Father, but we lived apart. He put a barrier between us. I had no understanding of why he did that, but I felt it and knew something was there. We had no emotional bond, and he displayed no interest in my development. My emotional connection was with Mother and YeYe. I did not know he suffered trauma from war."

When I read that Father intentionally deflected my anger onto himself to protect Mother, I was stunned. Seeing him protect her in this way made me view him in a different way, as an honorable man. I knew he loved her, and I began to view his efforts to get me out of China as an indication of his love for me, which he could never express.

"Winson. Are you okay?" Virginia's question brought me back into the present. I looked at her and nodded.

"I couldn't understand Father. We were so different. I never knew of the arrangement Mother made with him, or that he acted like it was his idea to send me to Canada when it was really Mother."

Virginia leaned over and hugged me. It took me a few minutes to regain my composure, then I continued reading:

> *Father made a beautiful calligraphy pen with several tips, and today we took it to Zhang with a letter for Wen Shun. He told me to use Wen Shun's new name on letters and asked for extra money to send the package.*
>
> *He finally gave me an address in Vancouver.*
>
> *It's been a bad day. I learned that the government is considering closing my school, and I do not know how we can survive without my salary. Father has fewer orders for musical instruments.*
>
> *I wish we all could have left with Wen Shun.*

I swallowed hard. "What's happened to my family?"

"We're doing what we can for now. We'll go through this together," Julian said.

I was thankful to be with Julian and Virginia, but my heart was broken.

That evening I read Caitlin Mr. Wong's letter, the journal pages, and the letter I wrote to Mother. "I don't understand why Father took the blame. I have been mad at him all these years."

"He was protecting your relationship with your mother. I think war causes people to do whatever they can to survive," Caitlin responded.

I could feel the anger I had harbored for years against my father releasing.

Then I read what I had not translated for Julian and Virginia, "*I desire that Wen Shun meets a family not of his flesh and blood, but of his heart.*"

That night Caitlin held me in her arms until I fell asleep.

Chapter Seventeen

"Sit across from me," Julian said as I pushed him into the office. "Ever since your first day working for me, you have taken care of me day and night, lifting me in and out of bed and my wheelchair, cleaning me, never giving me a look of displeasure even when I soiled myself and you. Whatever I needed, you provided with respect and never treated me as an invalid. Your demeanor and attitude mean more to me than you know, and you have never complained. I have often caught myself referring to you as my son. At first, I thought it was a slip. However, it was because, in every way except blood, you're a son to me."

He looked at the photos of his wife and Joseph on his desk, then looked at me, and his eyes turned watery.

"Julian, you know how much I respect you. It's an honor to care for you. You are family for me."

"This is hard for me to express." He hesitated and took several dry swallows. "Since Ruthie died, I tried to be there for Joseph, but it took all my energy to cope with my injuries, surgeries, and therapy. I was on heavy pain medication, and we argued every time we saw each other, then we lost touch."

His breathing became labored. It took a lot out of him to talk openly about his relationship with Joseph, and it was difficult for me to hear the pain in his voice and see it on his face.

"Winson, I love you as though you were my own son. If you're willing, I want to adopt you."

My heart pounded, and I wondered if I heard him correctly? Sponsorship was okay, but I was hesitant to be adopted because it would feel like closing the door to my past. I knew he missed his wife and son, but I realized this was more than an attempt to mitigate the pain from his son's death when I looked in his eyes.

"I'm overwhelmed."

"I hope that's a yes."

I thought of my family and whether Mr. Wong would find them. Would they be disappointed if I was adopted by a white family? I think they knew we would never see each other again and wanted the best for me.

When I thought of Mother's desire for a family of my heart and realized that I loved Julian almost as much as I did YeYe, I said, "Absolutely."

I hugged him and realized the tears on my cheeks were Julian's. I cradled his head, and it took some time to compose ourselves.

When we did, he said, "I want you to know that I have given much thought and consideration to what I have offered. I have asked you from my heart, but my head also tells me that you'll have better opportunities in the business world as my son, which leads me to my second question."

He locked eyes with me. "You've been carrying out my business decisions at the bank for years. You have been my connection to the staff, and there's no one I trust more than you. I want you to run the bank. I'll provide all the support you require for making decisions."

I tried to remain calm, at least on the outside.

"Will you accept the position of President of Merchants Bank and Trust?"

I never imagined the possibility of managing the bank, but would people in the community take offense to a Chinese running the bank, or employees feel passed over by my promotion?

"Julian, I'm moved and honored by your offer, but I'm concerned about the reaction from bank customers and employees. I filled in for a teller a few times, and some customers refused to be served by me."

I paused and looked away. "I'll carry out your wishes, but you must give further consideration to who should be president."

"This is the first you have told me of customer complaints. You have been terrific managing the bank for quite a while and now are more than qualified to head the organization. Business has been good, and we have not lost any customers. Remember, you taught me that whoever you care about becomes your family and that includes Virginia, Rhoda, Caitlin, and you."

My parents wanted me to have the opportunity to pursue a better life, but I was apprehensive about the consequences of this decision on Julian's business. How was I to respond? I didn't want to upset him by refusing.

"We're family, but have the right person, a Canadian, operate the bank."

"I don't want to force it on you, but I have plans I want to be completed, and you have the energy and fortitude to implement them. I realize this is a lot all at once for you. Why don't you talk with Caitlin."

"I'll certainly do that."

"It's been a long day. I'm fatigued and need to rest."

I fluffed his pillows, situated him in bed, and sat with him until he fell asleep.

I wrestled with both the adoption and the bank presidency he proposed. Regarding the adoption, was it conceivable that I'd ever return to my family in China with Mao in control? Would we find my family and bring them to Canada? Would they understand my adoption?

Regarding the presidency, I was still concerned about the community response of a Chinese being the bank's president.

I was honored by both offers, but Julian was right that Caitlin needed to be part of these decisions. That night when I told Caitlin about my conversation with Julian, she said, "You tend to make decisions on what's in the best interest of the other person. Think of it this way, if Julian is confident in your abilities and feels it's in his best interest for you to be president, you should trust his judgment."

She took my hand, looked at me with those puppy-dog eyes, and whispered, "You were meant to be with the people in your life, your family in China, then Kai and Jackson at the camp, Catherine, Julian and me in Collingwood, and we've all been there for you. Accept what's meant for you."

"Mother told me to go to Canada with all my heart and never look back. Since leaving home, I've had my slave name and number, which I put off like old clothes, to be replaced by a new suit, and now I'm wearing Julian's fine clothing."

"Your name doesn't matter as long as you remain the same."

"If Mr. Wong finds my family, do you think they'll be upset if Julian adopts me?

"I think your family loved you enough to send you to Canada for your protection. They wanted a good life for you, and Julian has offered that. I think they would be proud of who you have become."

Caitlin always gave me good advice.

⌇

Julian didn't say much through breakfast the next morning. He asked me to take him to his office, and when I situated him behind his desk, he asked me to sit.

"Have you and Caitlin discussed my offers?"

"We have, and she was very encouraging, which I should have expected." I sat up in my chair and pushed my feet into the ground. "In all respects, you have been a father to me, and I'm honored to be your son. Caitlin told me that I always consider the other person first and reminded me that I've been functioning as president with your support. So I accept the position and will do my best to live up to your expectations."

His face relaxed. "My son, you have made my day. Push me back, open the top left drawer, there's a manila envelope with my name and Clive's, open it, and pull out the papers."

I found the envelope and pulled out the pages.

"By the way, from now on, I want you to sit on this side of the desk. It's yours! Move me over, sit here, fill out those forms, and let me know if you need help."

After moving him and pulling up the desk chair, I looked at the document. Sitting behind his desk and seeing the adoption application overwhelmed me.

"There's more for us to discuss."

I looked up.

"Clive is Chairman of the Board, and I'll have him draw up the necessary documentation to officially make you President and Chief Executive Officer and a member of the Board of Directors.

"I have a vision for the future I want to share with you. I want to initiate a new assistance program providing seed loans to immigrants and minorities. I've been thinking of the early settlers who cleared land, put it into production, only to lose their properties due to lack of education or corruption. We'll work with my attorneys and consultants to create a financial assistance program, which I hope will become a model for the banking industry.

"I've directed Clive to establish a charitable trust to carry out projects in the community and am designating Clive and you as co-trustees. The first project is to build an arboretum to honor my wife and parents. They sacrificed so we'd have the opportunity to live as we do today in Canada and to remind people that as long as they persevere, they can overcome obstacles and reach their goals.

"Then I want to create a trust to fund synagogues in Collingwood, Meaford, and Owen Sound. I don't want those families who struggled to maintain our faith to be forgotten. I want to preserve their history. This may be part of the initial trust's funding, but Clive will make that decision."

I didn't know what all this entailed but was excited to be involved and carry out his vision. "Those are meaningful projects. I'll record notes from today in my journal, but now you need to rest."

"You're constantly a step ahead of me." It had been a long time since Julian had taken a step. Julian took delight in his unintended humor and started laughing.

"What is all the laughter about?" Virginia asked as she came into the room.

Julian tried to express his inadvertent humor but was so tickled that he continued giggling. When I told her, Virginia smiled and started chuckling, and it became contagious.

"I could hear the laughter all the way in the kitchen. What's going on?" Rhoda bellowed.

Between gasps of air, Virginia said, "Julian told Winson he's a step ahead of him, eh."

"Winson is always a step behind him, pushing the chair," Rhoda added. The laughter increased with the reality of her statement. Rhoda told me later it had been years since she'd heard Julian laugh.

When Julian set goals for himself and focused on the needs of others, it became therapy for his own situation.

Chapter Eighteen

We were successful in obtaining statements from Jeep and George. The timber inspector was reluctant to cooperate initially, but after disclosing testimony from Jeep and George, he agreed to a plea bargain and gave a sworn statement. Julian leaned on a representative who owed him a favor about reopening the investigation based on new evidence, interviews, and certified statements. The representative told Julian the probability to reopen an inquiry was good but also recommended not taking on Peabody-McCall due to its political influence.

In a meeting with Julian and Clive, it was agreed that Clive would meet with Simco Shipbuilding's CEO, Hollis Fitch, and present what we discovered, the potential for reopening the investigation, and for indictable offenses against the company.

When Clive returned from the meeting, he said, "Fitch categorically denied our discoveries. I told him motions could be filed through the criminal courts, and he said if we proceeded, they'd vigorously fight any charges and consider filing defamation lawsuits against us."

Julian replied, "Did you point out that a special commission could be appointed by the government to reopen the investigation? And the insurance companies, who paid out major settlements for losses to Simco, would likely file suits to recover paid out claims and sue for punitive damages if negligence on behalf of Simco was proved?"

"I did, but Fitch said they have community support based on the economic impact on the area. Then he gave a veiled threat that they have long memories and political connections that would make business as usual difficult for your bank and my law practice. I told him that everyone would need to do what they thought was right.

"He did offer an olive branch and said that all parties, including the community, would be better served if there would be a settlement. I asked what a settlement would look like, and he responded by asking what we would expect. I told him that settlement elements would require Simco Shipyard to provide a compensation fund for families impacted by the accident and fund an insurance reserve for such future occurrences and medical disabilities. Regarding Kierian Mulroney, provide back pay, a retirement package, payment for defamation, and a public apology clearing him of all accusations of negligence."

"How did he respond?" I asked.

"He'd consult with ownership and get back to us."

"What do we do now?" Julian asked.

"We wait."

❧

Three days later, Clive called. I took the phone to Julian and held it to his ear so we both could hear.

"Fitch told me to draft a memorandum of understanding that would provide for the settlement conditions we discussed."

Julian smiled.

"There were several additional conditions. Any agreement would be contingent on all records, information, and conversations of the negotiations remain confidential and sealed. Nothing is to be disclosed to the public."

"That's acceptable," Julian said.

"Simco Shipbuilding would agree to establish a fair and reasonable compensation fund and insurance reserve."

"That's acceptable."

"Provide Mulroney backpay, a severance package, and eligibility for retirement pay, but there would be no public apology or payment for defamation. I told Fitch I'd present his proposal for consideration."

Julian said, "I believe what we have achieved is in the best interest of the families who have been injured. Winson, it's up to you to meet with Mulroney. If he disagrees, we have no agreement, and those affected families won't receive any aid."

I had a coldness at my core. Without vindication, I couldn't see Kierian agreeing to this condition.

∽

I was apprehensive as Caitlin went with me to meet with her parents. Kierian sat in his chair, and Maureen was on the couch next to Caitlin as I reviewed the settlement negotiations and the offer that was made.

When I told Kierian he'd receive no public apology or defamation payment, he said, "I demand a public apology for what those sons of bitches did to me!"

Caitlin looked at me when Kierian said, "Bloody Hell! Maureen, bring me whiskey."

She gave him a displeasing look and walked to the kitchen. He hadn't taken a drink since the first night we ate together.

When she returned with a tall glass, he said, "I didn't ask you to wet the damn whiskey." Scowling at her, his face turned red as he banged the arm of the chair several times with his fist before bellowing, "I spent my life in that yard, gave them my best years, and this is how they treat me after busting my ass. They're cocksuckers!"

He lifted the glass, took a swallow, and jumped up shouting, "Son of a bitch Woman, this is tea!" and he threw it on her and yelled, "Bring me a pint of gat!" He grabbed his left arm, put his hand on the edge of the chair to steady himself, and plopped down like a sack of potatoes.

Both Caitlin and Maureen rushed to his side. Caitlin said, "Daddy, are you okay?"

He slowly nodded, and after several minutes of silence, I said, "Kierian."

When he didn't respond, I said it louder a second time and waited until he looked at me. "Are you willing to provide a public apology for what you did to Caitlin and me?"

Looking down, he gritted his teeth, pressed his lips together, slouched in the chair, and glanced about as if looking for an exit.

Then I added, "This agreement doesn't compensate Mr. LeBlanc for the loss of Joseph or me for Jackson's death."

He squirmed like a caged animal.

"But you're still alive and have your wife and daughter."

Caitlin said, "Daddy, think about all those women who lost their husbands and children who lost their fathers. This agreement will provide some compensation for them."

Maureen leaned over and whispered something into Kierian's ear.

"Tell the bastards, I agree."

Chapter Nineteen

1965

"I want to listen to music. Bring the record player and records from the closet behind my desk." Julian said to me one Saturday morning after I'd rubbed him with lotion and worked his muscles and joints.

"Which ones?"

"All of them. It's time we get culture in this house."

I enjoyed the lightness of his mood as I set up the player and put on a Beethoven record when Rhoda entered the room, attracted by Symphony No. 9 in D minor.

"What's going on here?" she boomed.

"Do you want to dance?" Julian quickly responded.

We were laughing, which drew Virginia into the room.

"What's happening?"

"Julian asked me to dance," Rhoda said with a big grin on her face.

The laughter coursed in rounds.

Julian laughed so hard his face turned red. When he caught his breath, he said, "Listen, it's about time I help you appreciate the finer things in life. When Ruthie and I lived in Meaford, we'd go to the opera. But the finest acoustics and the best talent is at the Orillia Opera House. Virginia, buy tickets for the next performance, we're all going to the opera. Ladies, you need to get evening gowns and include Caitlin. Winson, we need to fit you in one of my tuxedos. We're going to enjoy a night at the opera."

It was good to see this change in Julian. He appeared to be overcoming the emotional paralysis which gripped him since losing Ruth and Joseph. Over the following week, he was cheery and prodded the girls to find attractive formal dresses for the opera scheduled for the last Saturday in November. The three of them planned a shopping trip to Toronto, and a tailor came to the house and fitted tuxedos for Julian and me.

∽

A week later, it was a beautiful fall day. The maples were in a spectacular display of color, the air was crisp, and geese were squawking as they started their migratory trek to warmer climates.

It was a morning of the regular routine, Julian ate breakfast, I exercised his joints and gave him massage therapy, then he wanted to rest, and I positioned him in bed. Kai would arrive in thirty minutes.

I was walking out the door to go to the bank when Rhoda screamed, "Virginia, Winson, come quick, Julian's in distress."

When I entered his bedroom, Julian was gasping for air, in pain, and perspiring heavily. There was a strong urine smell, not unusual, but this was a foul odor. Virginia was at his side, taking his vitals. She asked me to give him oxygen while she called Dr. Gardner to describe his symptoms.

She finished the call, and the color went out of her face. "Dr. Gardner is calling for an ambulance. He thinks Julian might've suffered a heart attack. The next few hours will be critical."

Julian's skin was cold, and his eyes were lifeless. His body was under great duress. Time stopped for me while we waited for the ambulance. In a whisper, Julian called for Virginia. She bent over him, her ear next to his lips, with her hand she cradled the side of his head for a moment, then walked to the night table, picked up the picture of Julian with his wife, placed it on his chest, and whispered to him.

When she saw his lips move, she put her ear next to his mouth. Then she turned to me and said, he is calling your name.

I leaned over him and heard his faint voice repeating my name. My eyes filled with tears as I knelt on the floor next to his bed, held and kissed his hand. When I saw his color turn greyish, my anguish increased for the man who had become a father to me.

I spoke softly in his ear until the ambulance arrived then watched as two attendants in white uniforms entered the bedroom, checked his vitals, started an IV, lifted his motionless body onto a stretcher, and carried him out.

When I looked at the empty bed and soiled sheets, I noticed his slippers and carried them with me to the car. Following behind the ambulance with Virginia driving, none of us spoke as I watched the clock move minute by minute.

Caitlin, Rhoda, Virginia, and I were in the waiting room when a man and a woman in green gowns came out of the emergency room and approached us. "Are you Mr. LeBlanc's family?"

When I said, "I am his son, Winson LeBlanc," he paused for a moment, furrowed his brow, then extended his hand.

"I'm Dr. Tramer, and this is Leslie, my assistant. When we received your father, he was in severe cardiac arrest. We administered medications and shocked his heart several times, but he passed a few minutes ago. Please accept our sympathies."

We sobbed, and my heart ached. Over the last few months, he was happy and positive, wanting to go places and do things, establishing initiatives at the bank. His attitude and energy had turned around, and suddenly it was hard to believe Julian was gone.

Virginia took charge of planning Julian's funeral. She contacted Rabbi Schul, who said he'd be able to come in two days before Shabbat. He asked us not to leave Julian's body alone, so I went with him to Drott's Funeral Home.

Virginia ordered a simple pine box.

I asked Mr. Drott, "I'd like to clean and dress Julian and place him in his final repose. He's Jewish and won't be embalmed."

He looked over his glasses and said, "You wouldn't know what to do?"

"I worked here for a few months years ago."

He stared at me, then looked me up and down.

"I was here when your nephew Kelly left to go work at the shipyards."

"That was you, eh?"

"Yes, Sir."

"You look to have done well for yourself. As long as you keep this confidential, I'll allow it."

∽

I cried while washing Julian for the last time. I gently wrapped him in a white shroud. Before I covered his face, I kissed his forehead and rested him in the pine box. Then I put the picture of him with Ruth in the casket.

"Julian, you were a father to me in more ways than you'll ever know." I stopped because I needed a moment to collect myself, then I started again, "Father, I miss you."

As tears fell down my face, I said, "You were a wonderful man with a large heart that outgrew your body. I'll honor the work you have trusted me to carry on. When I hugged you, I felt your love, and it didn't matter that you couldn't hug back. We're family, and I'll miss you every day. I love you."

During the service, Rabbi Schul pointed to the closed casket and said, "Julian is dressed in a white burial shroud, tachrichim, which is purposely kept simple. We do this because there is no distinguishing between rich and poor in death, for we are dust, and unto dust we shall return. The blood of a person is considered as holy as his life and deserves a proper burial. From the moment of death, his body has not been left alone until it is placed in the ground. This practice is called *shemira*, or guarding, and is the way we honor the dead. Winson, Caitlin, Virginia, and Rhoda all stood vigilantly and took turns reading psalms with him for two days until I could be here for the burial. This man was loved by his family and this community."

Rabbi Schul tore his garment and recited a blessing, "Baruch atah Hashem Elokeinu melech haolam, dayan ha'emet," Blessed are you, Lord our God, Ruler of the universe, the true Judge. We recited the same blessing as witnesses, "Baruch dayan emet," Blessed is the one true Judge. The Rabbi then approached us and tore black ribbons to symbolize our loss.

Julian was carried out of the funeral home as we followed, reading the 23rd Psalm. At the cemetery, we stopped seven times as the casket was carried to the grave, and we recited Psalm 91. The coffin was lowered into the grave, then we each used the back of the shovel to completely cover it. The Rabbi repeated Psalm 91 and El MalehRachamim.

It's difficult to mark the death of a friend, a brother, a father. We all are equal in death. We should be equal in life.

Chapter Twenty

The following Monday morning, before leaving for the bank, I went into Julian's bedroom, looked at the pictures on the walls, and then walked to his bed to touch his pillow.

When I entered his office, I ran my hand across his desk, opened the desk drawer, lifted the mezuzah, kissed it, and put it in my pocket. I was crestfallen as I walked to the bank.

The staff was busy, preparing to open as I slipped into my office unnoticed. A few minutes later, Peggy stood in the doorway and said, "Good morning, Sir, may I have a word."

"Good morning, Peggy, please come in."

"My condolences to you and Caitlin on Mr. LeBlanc's passing and know that the staff and I mourn his loss with you. I have never been to a Jewish funeral. It was a beautiful service."

"Thank you for your kind words. I was surprised at how many people attended. He was beloved by this community."

"I'm sorry to bother you with business at a time like this, but several people have asked me about their jobs and the bank's future. All of us want to continue to work under you."

"Please assure them and any customers who may ask that as far as I know, nothing will change. Mr. LeBlanc was very prudent, and he had a succession plan for the bank."

"I'll miss him."

I bit my lip and sighed quietly, then said, "We'll all miss him."

After dinner that evening, Caitlin and I were in our sitting room. She took my hand, looked me in the eyes, and asked, "What's wrong?"

I told her about my conversation with Peggy and the staff's concerns.

"Did Julian discuss his plans for a transition of ownership of the bank with you?"

"No, he never brought it up." I pondered her question for a few moments. "Hopefully, Clive will know, he is chairman of the board. Or it will be in Julian's Will. To my knowledge, he has no family except his cousin, Benjamin Saez, and they didn't get along." I cleared my throat.

"Sweetheart, you look concerned."

"I never considered that I might lose my position at the bank. It'll depend on who assumes ownership." She took hold of my hand.

"Whoever it is will need you."

"And then there's the house," I said.

She got up from her chair, came from behind, hugged me, and whispered in my ear, "We can always move in with my parents."

Maybe she thought that was funny, but I certainly didn't.

That night I dreamed I was on a ship at sea that pitched, dipped, and tossed about, and I when I awoke, my clothes were soaked.

The next morning I received a call from Clive's secretary requesting my presence, along with Virginia, Rhoda, and Caitlin, for the reading of Julian's Will on Friday morning.

The four of us drove together, and Clive's secretary escorted us to the conference room and served tea.

Clive came into the room, greeted each of us, and said, "This isn't what any of us would've wanted, but this day will come for each of us.

"Julian and I spent a lot of time together when he moved to Collingwood to open the bank. We spent even more time together after his tragic accident. We learned about each other and developed a deep friendship woven together with in-depth discussions about the nature of integrity, religion, history, a shared joy in connecting people and ideas, and using money and influence to do good.

"Like all the best humans, Julian was not easily distilled. An inherently conservative man with an adventurous soul, he was a man very much of his place and time who held a deep appreciation for those whose personal cultures were quite different from his own.

"His dedication to making the world a better place was self-evident to anyone who crossed paths with him, whether he was directly influencing employees or customers, or bridging cultures. His humanity and enthusiasm were even more important than his entrepreneurial accomplishments. He endured the loss of his wife Ruth, his son Joseph, and the body of his youth. Rhoda, you and I are the only ones here who knew Julian before his accident, when he was full of energy and possessed a zest for life."

We were all very emotional as we talked about Julian and his life for several minutes. It was difficult trying to restrain my sorrow.

When there was a pause, Clive said, "Julian's passing is a significant loss to each of us and the community. Let's move to the reading of his Will.

Clive took a sip of water, cleared his throat, and read at a slow pace:

Last Will and Testament of Julian LeBlanc

Having no wife or natural-born children, my only surviving relative is a cousin, Benjamin Saez, and his family. For the purposes of this document, the court should consider that Saez and his family have predeceased me.

Paralyzed since the accident which took my beloved wife Ruth, I have depended on Virginia Cassidy, a trusted caregiver, and friend, whom I leave the sum of $150,000 to allow her to return to her home in Nova Scotia and provide for her retirement and lifestyle.

To my faithful and loyal friend, Rhoda Green, who has worked for me diligently and faithfully for over twenty-five years, I leave the sum of $150,000 for her to spend her days as she chooses. My desire is for her to spend it on herself, but it's given without restrictions.

To my adopted son, Winson LeBlanc, who showed me love and respect despite my disabilities, displayed sensitivity, compassion, loyalty, and care; I leave all my stock in Merchants Bank and Trust to manage operations in the manner I have taught him.

I leave my house to Winson and Caitlin LeBlanc, to provide a home for their family and the sum of $150,000 to provide for their welfare.

The balance of my estate I leave to the LeBlanc Charitable Foundation to complete the projects I have started. Clive Owen and Winson LeBlanc are co-trustees of the Foundation.

If anyone is left out of this Will, it is intentional and not inadvertent.

The bequests of the Will were a total surprise. Inheriting the house and bank stock were unexpected and unimagined. I told Virginia and Rhoda that they were 'family' and invited them to continue on for as long as they wanted. Virginia said she'd stay for several months to explore the Collingwood area, which she could not do while taking care of Julian. Rhoda said she'd rather see us than her husband during the day. It helped all of us to stay together for some time.

"We still have tickets for the opera next weekend, and Julian would want us to go, eh." Virginia said.

"Let's go shopping in Toronto tomorrow. We have dresses to buy for the opera." Rhoda added.

The ladies agreed, and I was delighted. I was counting my blessings. I had left Hangzhou as a 'paper son' and found a 'paper father,' no, a real father, in Julian LeBlanc.

Chapter Twenty-one

1966

"To be blind in this life is to suffer."

Catherine surprised me with her statement one Saturday while I was visiting. "How easy it would be to slip the bonds of this world. Death's a boundary where pain and discomfort can't go beyond."

These were unusual remarks coming from Catherine. "Are you okay?"

"I need to walk, please help me up."

She was unstable on her feet, so I took her arm, and as we walked the hallway, she gingerly led each step with her left leg, and her right dragged behind. When we got to the foyer, she said, "I'm dizzy and need to sit."

She grabbed both my arms with wavering hands and clutched them as though it was essential. I put my hands at her waist and carefully lowered her to a chair.

"Do you want water?"

"Please."

"Sit here, and I'll just be a minute."

Her face was pale, and her skin felt clammy. When I got to the kitchen, I called Virginia, explained what happened, and she rushed over. By the time I returned to Catherine with the glass of water, she was trembling.

When Virginia arrived, she quickly examined her, took her pulse, and asked, "What are you feeling?"

"I'm dizzy and unstable on my feet. My left arm has tingled since yesterday. I didn't think it was anything, but it hasn't gone away."

"Catherine, we need to get you to the hospital and have Dr. Gardner examine you. Are you okay with that?"

Staunch and sturdy, I expected her to say no, but when she said, "We'd better go quickly," I became more alarmed.

I stayed with Catherine as Virginia went into the kitchen to call Dr. Gardner. When Virginia returned, she whispered to me, "She has heart symptoms. We need to hurry."

Julian had died of a heart attack just a few months earlier, I was fearful that Catherine was about to experience a similar event. Catherine didn't want an ambulance, so we drove in Virginia's car. After tests were run, Dr. Gardner approached us in the waiting room and said, "Catherine has suffered a mild heart attack. She's stable and resting comfortably, but we want to keep her here for a few days for observation."

Caitlin had been in Toronto all week completing her Degree at the Royal Conservatory of Music. When I called her from the hospital and told her what happened, she rushed to be with us.

One of us stayed with Catherine in the hospital until she returned home a week later. Virginia suggested we move her in with us, but Catherine refused. Virginia, Caitlin, and I alternated being with her so she could be in her own room. Caitlin taught piano to Catherine's students, and we looked for someone who could stay with Catherine for part of the day and prepare meals for her.

One morning Rhoda said, "I saw Wei Lei at the market yesterday, and she said that Mrs. Metzger accused her of stealing from Cott's and filed a police report so it would be of record. That Metzger lady is cruel!"

"What's she doing for work?" I asked.

"She's looking for jobs cleaning houses or cooking."

"We should have her stay with Catherine."

Rhoda put her hand on her hip and proclaimed, "Wei Lei can cook for Catherine, but not that congee stuff you make." Then she stomped her foot, pointed at me, and started laughing. She always liked to tease me when I made congee.

I talked to Kai, then went to see Wei Lei at her home. When she answered the door and saw me, she opened the screen door and whispered in Mandarin, "Let's talk outside, I don't want my parents to hear our conversation."

I was alarmed by how drawn she appeared. I followed her around the back of the house, and before I could say anything, she started crying.

I offered her my handkerchief, and when she regained her composure, I spoke softly, "Rhoda told me you were fired by Mrs. Metzger. Tell me, what happened?"

She wiped her face and said, "From my first week of work, Mrs. Metzger derided me and constantly criticized my work even though the customers complimented me. Her husband was frequently in the back and would drink a lot, you could smell it on him."

She choked up, fidgeted with her dress, then cleared her throat.

"I never liked the way he looked at me." When she bit her lip, I thought there was more to what she was sharing, but I needed to let her talk.

"Both of them spoke against minorities."

"I don't know how to ask, so forgive me, but did her husband touch you or make sexual advances?"

Flushed, she lost her composure and started sobbing.

I held her until she calmed down. I was anything but calm and wanted to punch Jay in the face.

She collected herself, stepped away from me, and said firmly, "You cannot tell Kai, he would do something to Mr. Metzger, and that would be the end of us. You cannot mention it to the police or anyone else, do you understand me?"

"It stays between us."

"He was always staring at me, looking me up and down, making rude comments about my body, and he touched me whenever he walked by. I was afraid of him, tried not to make eye contact, and ignored him as best I could. On my last day on the job, Mrs. Metzger walked in the back as her husband was forcing himself on me. She yelled, 'You're fired, and I'm filing a police report for the money you have been stealing from me.' Then she told me to get out. As I was leaving, I could hear her screaming at her husband.

"I never stole any money. I needed the job but was always afraid of Mr. Metzger and tried to avoid him. He had been drinking that day and grabbed me. I was pushing him away when she walked in. They are both evil, and that woman has eyes of hate."

"I have experienced that from Mrs. Metzger."

"Several days after I was fired and while Kai was working at Mr. LeBlanc's, a horrible policeman named Ellarby came to our home to investigate the charges. He looked around our house, opening everything he could, looking for something, asked my parents questions, and when they couldn't speak English, he kept raising his voice as if that would help them understand what he was asking. When Mother started crying, he asked me about the legality of their citizenship. He rudely yelled at her to shut up and then said he would report them to immigration."

As the tears cascaded down her face, I put my finger to my lips and then to hers and said, "I know about Ellarby and will have my attorney contact the Chief of Police and work to get the charges dropped."

She nodded. "Thank you for being so kind."

"And I have a job for you."

She hugged me and, through her tears, said, "You are sunshine in our lives. Kai has spoken about how you have looked after him." Then she kissed me on the cheek.

That afternoon, she started staying with Catherine, and when she cooked that evening, she made enough for all of us, including Mr. Lawrence. After a week of her meals, Mr. Lawrence hired her to clean the house and cook for him.

Clive contacted the Chief of Police, who said there was insufficient evidence to charge Wei Lei and that Ellarby did not report her parents to immigration. When I told Wei Lei, she looked at me with a smile that lit up her entire being.

After a month, Mr. Lawrence offered the loft to Kai and Wei Lei in exchange for cleaning and cooking and Kai maintaining the house and gardens. They agreed, and this situation provided care for Catherine and allowed Wei Lei and Kai to move out of her parents' house.

I did not betray Wei Lei's confidence even though I wanted Jay Metzger to be punished. Some things you just don't want to keep hidden, but you have no choice but to do so.

One afternoon Caitlin called me at the bank to say that Catherine wanted to see both of us together. When I arrived, she sat in her chair in the parlor, wearing her favorite sweater and knitting while Caitlin sat next to her. I was surprised at how frail Catherine appeared. It was the first time she had been out of her room in weeks.

I pulled up a chair and sat next to her. "Hi Catherine, are you feeling okay?"

She nodded, rubbed her fingers over my mother's jade pendant, then reached for both our hands. "Winson and Caitlin, the two of you are so close to my heart that I consider you my children." She coughed, and I handed her my handkerchief. "Music has always filled the empty spaces in my life, but as I walk into the autumn of my life, I am grateful for the two of you.

"I asked you here to tell you that they performed many tests when I was in the hospital. I was fortunate that you took me when you did because they were able to put me on proper medication before I suffered a major heart attack. When I asked the doctors to tell me directly about my condition, they said I have a weakened heart, and I'm retaining fluid, which causes my legs to swell and reduces the blood flow to my kidneys. That all contributes to my weakness and dizziness. There is no cure, but I can manage it by reducing stress and changing my diet."

We were stunned. Caitlin put her arm around Catherine and said, "We love you and are here to help you any way we can."

Catherine squeezed my hand.

"Most of us want to avoid discussing death, but I view it as a departure. Death has a way of slowly creeping up on us until it becomes an interruption in our lives, like an uninvited guest. But rather than avoiding it, I choose to accept and embrace it gracefully."

I caressed her hand. Caitlin was holding back tears. We had just lost Julian, and I was not prepared to lose Catherine.

"History teaches us that nothing lasts forever. But I do intend to put it off as long as possible."

"I'm glad to hear that. We want you with us for a long time, and I have some books to read to you." I said.

"I'm a private person." She paused to clear her throat. "I want to share parts of my life with you that I haven't revealed to others. Winson, I have told you part of my story, but I want to add to it with Caitlin here. Listening is a rare quality you both possess, so I want you to know my story."

Taking a deep breath, Catherine started. "My parents, Holly and Andre DeVeaux, were married in the Alsace region of France. Papa was eight years younger than Mama. The economy was stagnant in the 1880s, so they emigrated to Canada in 1890, seeking an opportunity, as did many other Europeans. They settled in Quebec in 1892, where Papa worked in a bank, and Mama was a pianist and gave music lessons. Money was tight, so they moved to Collingwood and lived with Aunt Florence and Aunt Dorothy until Papa found work as a purser on a ship. Mama bore three children, Forrest was their firstborn in 1895, I was born in 1899, and Thomas was born in 1907. Thomas died when he was three.

"Papa worked hard, and Mama was frugal. From years as a purser aboard a ship, he acquired a taste for the luxuries in life, but Mama resented the long stints at sea and his new spending habits. When Forrest died in 1928, my parents became estranged.

"When I was old enough, I went to boarding school at the Canadian National Institute for the Blind, and when a music teacher came in to teach piano, I discovered my life's passion. Papa became obsessed with doing all he could to advance my skill, and I thrived and sought advanced training at the Royal Conservatory of Music in Toronto. When I won an international competition at the Canadian National Exhibition, it led to a tour in Europe with concerts in Paris, London, and Jerusalem. Papa accompanied me on all my travels.

"During this time, Mama became infirm and was taken care of by her sisters, she died unexpectedly while we were in Europe, and Papa died a month later. Without him, traveling became difficult, and that's when I realized it was time to return to Collingwood and concentrate on teaching rather than performing.

"When I started touring, Papa purchased this house and rented it out. When he died, he willed the house to me with instructions for the attorney to sell it and retain a life estate so I could reside rent-free until my death. The house was sold to Mr. Lawrence with those stipulations."

Caitlin and I looked at each other with surprise.

"My passion is teaching piano. I know I'm a taskmaster and demanding when on the clock giving lessons, but I loved all my students, and you two were special. Winson, I loved it when you read to me and offered to run errands, but I treasure the time we spent together the most."

She reached for both my hands. When I gave them to her, she gripped them tightly and didn't let go. Catherine was dear to me. She filled the void in my heart for my mother. My voice was trembling as I said, "You understood me better than I understood myself. Until Caitlin, you were the only one who could open my heart, and you encouraged me to change in innumerable ways."

Caitlin added, "You have been an inspiration to me, and your teaching and encouragement have made such a difference in my life. I'm grateful for all of the opportunities you have given me, and without you, I would not have completed my degree at the Royal Conservatory."

I could see the tears well up in Caitlin's eyes as I said, "Caitlin and I wouldn't have met, nor would we be together now if it weren't for you."

"You two were meant for each other." Catherine smiled and squeezed my hands. Caitlin's eyes glistening as she winked at me and put her hands on Catherine's and mine.

Catherine cleared her throat. "The Mayor called me a week ago. The city wishes to honor me with the Order of Collingwood for my musical contribution to the people of this fine city and in recognition of my participation in various concert tours in Europe and North America. The City Council wants me to attend the ceremony, and they invited an old friend, Yves Marceau, for the presentation." She stopped, cleared her throat, and her hand began to tremble.

"Yves was a composer who I played duets with while on tour. We became close, remarkably close, and he wanted to marry me. I loved him, but there were other considerations."

She paused, her lower lip jutted out, and her face saddened. "I wouldn't have been a capable wife and mother, and my focus was on my career and Papa, so I broke off the relationship, but he continued to write me letters for years. I can't stop him from attending the ceremony, but I'm struggling with seeing him."

She spoke so pragmatically about her relationship with Yves, and when Caitlin looked at me, we were both surprised at what Catherine shared. "What can we do to help?" I asked.

"During the ceremony, they're going to announce a program to honor my work called *Play this Piano*. They're going to place pianos on the street so that anyone walking along the sidewalks can play them. This was an idea I presented to the city council years ago to promote music appreciation in Collingwood."

"What a marvelous idea! I'm so glad they're honoring you this way," Caitlin said.

"I'm pleased they liked my idea but stressed about Yves. I received a letter from him yesterday saying he accepted the city's invitation and wants to spend time with me."

She choked up and dropped her head.

"I could not sleep last night. He represents a chapter in my life I don't want to reopen. Emotionally, I don't know if I can handle seeing him."

"What happened to Yves after you broke up?" Caitlin asked.

"He became a successful composer and never married. I would've been a handicap to him and didn't want to impede his career, so I wrote him a letter after our separation, telling him I could never be the woman he deserved."

Her heart was so tender and fragile.

"We're here for you. We'll be with you at the dedication and, if you want, when you meet Yves," Caitlin told her.

"I'm struggling with all this attention, and two months from now, I don't know if I'll be alive or that my health will allow me to attend the ceremony. If I'm unable to attend, would you two accept the award on my behalf?"

Squeezing her hand, Caitlin replied, "We'd be honored, but our prayer is for you to be well enough to be there in person."

∞

When the time came for Catherine to receive the Order of Collingwood, she had an upper respiratory infection and was advised to stay home. Caitlin and I attended the ceremony to accept the award on her behalf.

In my acceptance for her, I thanked the audience and said, "If she hadn't been blind, she would've enjoyed an incredible worldwide music career, and Collingwood would've missed out on her contribution and the impact she's had on so many lives in this community. I personally would've missed knowing one of the most important people in my life."

After the ceremony, a tall, distinguished-looking older man, dressed in an elegant dark grey suit, approached us. He had silver and black hair, high cheekbones, and penetrating blue eyes.

"I'm Yves Marceau, a long-time friend of Catherine's. We worked together on concert tours in Europe, and I've come a long way to see her again."

"It's a pleasure meeting you," Caitlin said.

"Catherine told us about your friendship. She's been sick and was advised by her doctor to stay home," I added.

Yves pulled out a pocket watch, opened it, and showed it to us. "This is a picture of my beautiful..." He paused as he choked up. "It's with me at all times."

It was a picture of Catherine, young and beautiful.

"She was stunning." His voice quivered.

"I leave for France in a few days. I came here thinking this may be my last opportunity to see her. She's dear to my heart, so please, would you take me to her?"

Respecting Catherine, I paused to consider his request. "I need to get Catherine's permission, but I'll do what I can to arrange it."

"I'm staying at the Collingwood Inn. When you ask, please tell her I love her."

༜

Caitlin and I gave Catherine the Order of Collingwood plaque, told her about the ceremony and meeting Yves, and his request.

She remained silent.

When Caitlin looked at me, I nodded, and then she said, "He still loves you and flies home in a few days. He came a long way to see you, and this may be your last opportunity to meet."

She paused for several minutes, and I could see her going through an internal struggle. "Bring Yves for a brief visit tomorrow morning."

I called Yves and told him to meet us in the parlor of the Lawrence House the next morning.

༜

He looked nervous as we escorted him into Catherine's room. She was in bed and under medication. The sheet was pulled up to her neck, her eyes lids fluttered, and she looked frail.

Yves's eyes were liquid as he sat in a chair next to her, and in a low tone, said, "My sweet Catherine, my love…"

Caitlin tugged at my hand, and we left them alone.

After Yves departed, we stayed with Catherine. She said, "We promised to write letters, and I'm glad I consented to see him."

She was visibly touched by his visit, and we didn't want her to be alone, so we read to her and played her favorite music. That night her breathing was rapid and shallow, and she had a persistent cough. When we called Virginia and explained the symptoms, she came and examined her for pneumonia and then called Dr. Gardner, who prescribed medications. Virginia gave her aspirin and pills to help her sleep and told us to have her drink plenty of fluids. We took turns sleeping, and one of us was by her side throughout the night.

Near four in the morning, she started shivering, and I helped her put on her favorite sweater. As I did for Julian, I hugged and rocked her until she finally calmed and fell asleep. Then I kissed both her cheeks and repositioned the blanket.

The next morning, I found a recording of Barber's Adagio for Strings in Julian's collection and played it for her and Caitlin on the phonograph.

Catherine said, "This piece is full of pathos and cathartic passion. Over the summer of 1936, Barber, Yves, and I toured Europe together, and we became good friends. Barber was in his twenties when he composed the work that summer, and he asked us to publicly perform the Adagio for the first time. That was the last time Yves and I performed together."

There wasn't a dry eye in the room. During lunch, she asked Caitlin to read Camus to her.

Chapter Twenty-two

Chills went up my spine when I collected Saturday's mail and recognized Mr. Wong's familiar envelope. I had continued to pay the retainer Julian established, but news from the search for my family had been so infrequent that I had put it out of my mind. Seeing the envelope, I realized that I needed to inform Mr. Wong of Julian's passing but that our engagement would continue under the same terms.

Since Caitlin was teaching piano and would not be home for several hours, I thought this would be a good time to read Mr. Wong's report. After preparing tea, I sat at Julian's desk and took his ivory letter opener with the inlaid onyx in my hand and slit the envelope.

As I rubbed my fingers on the paper, I imagined him sitting across from me in his wheelchair, with his compassionate eyes and familiar smile radiating his love and affection for me.

Before opening the folded pages, I closed my eyes and wondered what I would read. Would there be more of Mother's yellowed journal pages? I longed to see more of her thoughts in writing. In Mr. Wong's last letter, he thought she was isolated in the mountains teaching peasants and banned from returning to a city, but he was hopeful of finding her.

I let out a long sigh and pulled two pages from the envelope. There was nothing of Mother's journal, and I had a sinking sensation in my chest as I read.

Dear Mr. LeBlanc,

Conditions in China continue to be difficult, but we do not lose hope in finding Winson's family. Pai discovered that Winson's father was moved from a work camp after serving seven-years and is in Shanghai and lives in a state-run chemical factory, with the goal of uniting punishment and reformation to turn him into a law-abiding citizen. State-run facilities of this type notoriously have poor conditions. Prisoners are held under constant supervision and sleep in over-crowded conditions often in rusty iron bunks with minimal provisions for comfort. They are lucky to have even a single blanket and a thin mattress. Sometimes more aggressive prisoners take what little others have and use it for themselves.

With your permission, we will contact the authorities and attempt to negotiate his release. I need to request additional money because Pai paid extra for Winson's father's information. My invoice is enclosed.

If Winson wants to write a letter to his father, it should be brief and contain little personal information. We will attempt to get it to him.

We have been unable to gather additional information regarding Winson's mother and sister. Pai is working with new sources to find them. There is still no record of Winson's YeYe, even though he was a well-known Hangzhou craftsman. When I have more information, I will write again.

Sincerely,

Howard Wong

As I reread the letter, guilt flooded my emotions because I lived in luxury in Canada, and my family was trapped and separated, somewhere in Mao's China. I needed air and time to think so I walked to the harbor.

Seeing all the beautiful flowers in the yards, I thought of Caitlin's words to me, "You were meant to be with the people in your life, first your family in China, and now your family in Collingwood. We've all been there for you. Accept what's meant for you."

But what was meant for me?

Mother told me to go to Canada with all my heart and never look back. I had struggled for years remembering, and now, of all my family, the only person Mr. Wong and Pai could locate was my father. The man who neglected me as a son but took the blame for sending me away to protect Mother.

Could I turn my back on him?

When I returned home, I picked up Catherine's tattered copy of Camus' *The Plague*. As I rubbed the cover of the book that had meant so much to Caitlin and me, I pulled out the folded letter Catherine had me write to Father many years ago about the tension that had existed between us. I read it and realized how much my thinking had changed over the years, then took a paper from the top drawer of the desk and wrote Father a letter.

Father,

From an early age, I looked up to you and tried to honor you with my behavior. I admired your passion, how you stood for what you believed in, and were willing to fight for those causes. I respect you and want to take care of you as you age.

> *I am grateful to you and Mother for sending me to Canada. It was a struggle at first but I am happily married now and have a good job. I am so thankful to know you are alive. I have searched but been unable to find Mother, Lijuan, and YeYe.*
>
> *With warmest affection,*
>
> *Tao Wen Shun*

Then I wrote a cover letter to Mr. Wong inquiring about the probability of getting my father released and out of China. I also gave him information about Kai's parents and what additional retainer he needed to search for them.

Life is full of unexpected turns. Of all the people I hoped to find, the one I was most distant from is who was located. Maybe he needed me the most.

Chapter Twenty-three

It had been a challenging year. Time seemed to go by slowly as I mourned Julian's death and dealt with the bank's transition, assuring employees and customers the bank would continue to operate with the same integrity and values of its founder.

The LeBlanc Charitable Foundation was established, and Clive and I oversaw operations as trustees. We hired retired Royal Canadian Air Force Colonel Forrest Works as executive director to carry out Julian's directives on a daily basis.

∽

The fourth month after his death, auditors from the *Ministry of Finance* made an unannounced visit to the bank to conduct a full audit. Spending an entire week, they meticulously examined our books and files. This was unexpected, and I was worried.

When I contacted Clive and asked if this was customary, he made a few inquiries and called that evening. "My contacts told me this is unusual, but not without precedent. It's best to be compliant, answer all their questions, and provide full disclosure."

Caitlin asked, "What did Clive say?"

"To cooperate fully, and he assured me that everything we have done was proper, but I feel there is a hidden agenda."

"What do you think it is?" she asked.

"Banking authorities could be attempting to challenge the transfer of ownership or to uncover regulatory violations that might provide cause to revoke our bank charter."

"How can they do that?"

"I don't know, I can only speculate, but the Finance Minister manages the banking affairs of the country and has final authority. The examiners investigated over 200 of our customer accounts and left a questionnaire to be answered by any non-Canadian depositors, then left without comment or discussion."

Over the next few weeks, sleeping was difficult for both of us, and I suffered from unsettling dreams.

∞

One afternoon I received a Certified Letter from the *Commission on Citizenship and Immigration* requesting my attendance in two weeks at a meeting on Parliament Hill in Ottawa.

Enclosed were several forms to complete. As I read through the papers, the questions were asking for: home of origin, specific information on Tao Wen Shun, Zhu Yao, and Tao Winson, Port of Entry into Canada, documentation on my citizenship, sponsoring family, work history, family, next of kin, and additional questions of this type.

As I was filling out the paperwork, Caitlin sat next to me and put her hand on my arm. I looked at her soft blue eyes and said, "I'm concerned about the information requested in this letter and unnerved that they identified my name in China and my paper family name."

Her brow furrowed, and she straightened as she asked, "Are they attempting to deport you to China?"

"I don't know."

"Are they challenging your ownership of the Bank?"

"I'm certain they'd prefer having a Canadian citizen of Anglo or French descent run the bank. My ownership came through unusual circumstances."

"They can't remove you just because you're a Chinese man."

"They can do what they consider to be in the best interest of Canada and the Province of Ontario."

"You have demonstrated good conduct ever since you arrived in Canada, and you're a legally adopted Canadian citizen. Could it be motivated by what Julian did to gain a settlement with Simco Shipbuilding?"

"I have considered that."

Caitlin said, "I'm disappointed with my government."

I took a deep breath and felt empty. We were silent until Caitlin said, "Governments should be ruled by laws, and a ruling body of men shouldn't arbitrarily determine a man's future."

"But men interpret and carry out the laws."

She looked away, and we uncomfortably shifted our postures.

"What would happen to us if you were returned to China?"

I was confused and didn't know how to respond, and I privately thought I would face what Father or Mother experienced.

She looked like she was about to faint when she said, "Would they let me go with you?"

I held her in my arms and whispered, "Everything will be okay." It was my effort to be cheerful in stark contrast to my sense that something was not right.

She declared, "I would not let you go."

She hugged me as her tears fell on my shoulder. I had no thoughts, just numbness, and couldn't imagine facing my family's fate if the Canadian government returned me to China. But what I did know for sure was that I would not allow Caitlin to come with me if I was deported.

∽

I wanted to be positive but had trepidation over the forces originating these activities. I made sure everything was in proper order at the bank and that the staff was efficient and responsible, but I continued to be apprehensive. News travels, and there was speculation around the community regarding the audit examination and bank ownership by a Chinese man.

For several nights, Caitlin tossed and turned, struggling to sleep. The next morning, I said, "Sweetheart, let's focus on what we can control and prepare for the train trip to Ottawa. You take care of packing, and I'll focus on the requested records."

I didn't tell Caitlin, but there was also a request for proof of ownership regarding the transfer of the deed to Julian's house and stock in the bank.

It was daunting to have received a certified letter and questionnaire asking for information on my family in China, the status of relatives in Canada, dates, contacts, and more information than I had knowledge of. The request's timing was bothersome in that Julian had died, transferred bank ownership to me, and now the legality of my immigration was being investigated.

I went to Clive for advice and recounted the events since Julian's passing.

Clive said, "The fact you entered the country illegally shouldn't be an issue after your sponsorship and adoption. You are a legal citizen of Canada, and you have proved you're a hard-working, contributing citizen to Canadian society. I wish I could tell you what the Commission's questions will be, but I'm sure you will answer them honestly and professionally. I will provide the legal documentation needed for proof of citizenship, adoption, and transfer of title by Julian's *Last Will and Testament*. Just be the man of character that I know you are."

"Thank you for your confidence in me, Clive." I hoped I didn't show the angst I felt.

"I'll always tell you what I think, just like I did with Julian. This certainly isn't the turn of events we would have desired. I respect you for being honest and forthright.

"With all you have endured, I would like to do something special for you and Caitlin. I know the manager of the Chateau Laurier Hotel. He owes me a favor, so I'll book a room for you and Caitlin. It's walking distance to Parliament Hill and something I want to do for the two of you." Clive's warm smile was reassuring.

"Thank you for your kind offer. I appreciate your kindness and counsel. When Julian died, I lost my father and mentor, and I need him now, but…" I choked up and couldn't finish.

"I know, and I am here to support you."

I left his office with the feeling that he was troubled over how these circumstances would play out.

◈

Since receiving the notice to appear before the Ottawa Commission, I had lost weight. I tried hiding my concerns from

Caitlin, but the challenge of my immigration to Canada was consuming me. If I was deported back to China or somewhere else, I worried about what would happen to Caitlin.

As if that wasn't concerning enough, there was a growing anti-communist sentiment in the government that targeted the Chinese. Would the government perceive bank ownership by a Chinese man as a national security threat?

Newspaper editorials parodied Orientals as looking different, practicing different customs, and associated us with Mao. A small minority of Chinese in Canada were openly communists, mostly university students, and their activities always made the news.

I visited Catherine, who was feeling much better and had resumed teaching several students a day. She assured me I wouldn't be deported and expressed confidence that Julian had taken all the necessary and appropriate steps to ensure the transfer of ownership of the bank stock and the house were legal and would hold up in a court of law.

It helped to be with her, but I had to continue reminding myself that I was a legally adopted citizen of Canada and could not be deported.

∽

Early on a Sunday morning, Caitlin prepared breakfast, then picked at her food as we sat at the table. We moved to the porch to enjoy our tea and talked. I knew she was stressed over the trip, so I said, "You didn't eat much this morning."

"For the last few weeks, I have felt worn-out. I thought it might be an emotional reaction to what was transpiring with the bank, but then my breasts have been tender, and I missed my period."

I wasn't sure I heard correctly. I thought about it for a moment, perhaps longer than I realized, because Caitlin asked, "Winson, did you hear what I said?"

I smiled at her and said with as much love as I could manage, "Sweetheart, if that's what I think it means, I'm overjoyed."

She reached for my hand. I didn't want my reaction to be disappointing, but my mind flooded with questions and concerns. Was the miss from stress or a one-off occurrence, or our first child? If I was deported and she was pregnant, she'd have to raise our child by herself. Could she earn enough to support them both? But I couldn't allow my emotions to leak out and be displayed to Caitlin. If she was pregnant, the timing was cruel.

She interrupted my stream of thoughts, "Winson, are you upset?"

I said softly, "There's been so much happening that I'm overwhelmed. I'm proud to be your husband, and I look forward to having a child together."

"Well, we need to wait and see."

"Should we see the doctor?"

"Not yet."

I rose from my chair, got down on my knees next to her, held both her hands, looked into her beautiful blue eyes, and said, "I want to take each step together in this wonderful journey we're beginning."

Chapter Twenty-four

Both Caitlin and I were tense as we boarded the train for Ottawa, dreading the bureaucratic confrontation awaiting us. I tried to lighten the mood by joking, "I just realized this is my first train ride as a paying passenger." Caitlin looked at me and tried to smile, but her eyes showed nothing but apprehension.

Soon after we stowed our luggage and took our seats, the train whistle blew twice, then pulled out of the station. As it rumbled down the tracks, we were both lost in our own thoughts as we stared in silence out the window at the passing acres of wheat, corn, potatoes and fruit trees. As we approached an area near Algonquin, the terrain turned mountainous with giant trees and placid lakes. Caitlin pointed out the water lilies in the ponds, and I was impressed with the forces of nature, which carved these valleys, mountains, and high plateaus.

We enjoyed an excellent meal in the dining car, served by courteous and efficient black waiters. I remembered the train ride with Jackson and Kai from Vancouver to Collingwood, so after eating, I asked the waiter for food to take back to my car. Caitlin smiled as I took the tray and walked to the rear of the train, where a black porter stopped me and said, "Sir, this is as far as you can go."

"I'd like to go to the baggage car."

"Sorry, Sir, you aren't allowed."

"What's your name?"

"Please, Sir, just call me George."

"I mean your real name. What do the other porters call you?"

"Wash, Sir. It's short for Washington."

"Wash, do you know a porter named Ray Morris?"

"Yes, Sir!"

"I want you to take this tray of food to the baggage car, and you'll know what to do with it."

"Thank you, Sir. What's your name?"

"Winson. Ray helped me many years ago, and when you see him, tell him Winson said hello."

Returning to my seat, Caitlin had fallen asleep. I sighed deeply, closed my eyes, retraced my journey from Hangzhou to this point in time, and thought of how an immigrant always faces a paradox of optimism tainted by worry and fear. Often fleeing upheavals of war and persecution, he seeks out those countries with a need for workers. Borders open and close based on Immigration policies, which reflect supply and demand conditions.

We arrived in Ottawa in the late afternoon, and I was stunned by the scale of the railroad depot which looked like a modern-day Pantheon, with its cavernous sandstone walls and towering columns that supported a coffered ceiling.

Clive reserved a room for us at the Chateau Laurier Hotel, across the street from the train station and one block from Parliament Hill and Confederation Square. We were awestruck by the grandeur of the castle-like hotel, and I couldn't shake the feeling that staying in a hotel like this was the last kindness we would enjoy before I would be deported. Nonetheless, I was appreciative of his gesture and thankful that Caitlin could enjoy a lavish room.

As we walked up the steps to the hotel, a white-gloved footman looked me up and down and glanced back toward a bellman wearing a long red coat and black hat. My past experiences caused me to expect the worst, so I mentally prepared what I would say when we were turned away.

The bellman bellowed, "Welcome to the Chateau Laurier. My name is William." Turning to the footman, he said, "Please assist this nice young couple with their bags and escort them to the reception desk." William bowed and said, "Enjoy your stay," as Caitlin squeezed my hand and flashed a radiant smile at William, who doffed his hat.

We were received and checked in by a courteous front desk receptionist, who informed us that the changing of the guard ceremony was to occur at six that evening in front of the Capital and thought it would be an enjoyable event for us. A liveried bellman escorted us to our room, which was huge and elegantly decorated. We unpacked, refreshed ourselves, put on comfortable shoes, and headed to Parliament Hill, where the grounds were like a park with three magnificent government buildings. Centre Block was the largest building and ran parallel to Wellington Street, and its focal point was a four-faced clock tower above the entry that chimed every fifteen minutes. The other two buildings were perpendicular to Center Block and called West and East Blocks.

I was overcome by the stateliness and expanse of the capital setting. The buildings were of Gothic architecture, built of different stone types and situated on a bluff overlooking the Ottawa River's surging waters and the Rideau Canal, which we could see from our hotel window. As we walked the grounds, my thoughts were interrupted by a strange sound.

Caitlin saw my puzzled look, laughed, and told me it came from bagpipes, a traditional instrument in Ireland and Scotland. As the noise got louder, we looked to our right and saw a ceremonial guard parading up the street. The bagpipers wore skirts, which Caitlin called kilts.

Behind the bagpipers was a marching band from the Regiment of Canadian Guards. The band members wore black pants, long buttoned red coats, and black Cossack hats about a foot tall. I wanted to enjoy the music with Caitlin but was distracted by thoughts of the hearing. Caitlin must've known because she kept squeezing my hand as we watched the ceremony.

I was to appear before the Commission the next morning in East Block, so we returned to the hotel as soon as we had supper and went to bed. At three in the morning, Caitlin trembled from a dream, and I woke her gently and held her until she went back to sleep. Then my mind became active, and I couldn't sleep, so I quietly climbed out of bed, tucked the covers around my beautiful wife, and thought of the upheaval of recent events, which instead of pulling us apart, drew us closer.

After dressing in warm clothes, I left the hotel and walked through empty streets toward Parliament Hill and across the bridge spanning the canal. I sat on a bench at the end of the bridge and looked up at the stars in a moonless, cloudless night. It reminded me of the dark nights at sea.

My mind returned to the request for background information regarding my paper family name. What disturbed me was how the Commission knew about the false name I used to enter the country? Where did they obtain it? Did it come from Dung or Tak?

Would my 'paper son' documentation be a problem for my citizenship. If I returned to immigrant status and was deported, what would become of our marriage, and what would my life be like if I returned to China?

It seemed that an immigrant was always up against some impenetrable caste system, and yet everybody is an immigrant at a point in the past. Citizenship should be judged on a man's values, principles, and ideals, not by the color of his skin or where he was born.

All of my affairs had been conducted legally, except for my entry into the country. My parents could bear witness to my story, but were unable to testify on my behalf.

In my youth, I was naïve of the forces at work in China and the world, such as hate, prejudice, envy, and excessive ambition. I lived a simple life back home, but based on Mr. Wong's letters, there was no home to return to. Circumstances beyond my control had cost me years of my youth and my family.

Because I would interact with lawyers and politicians over the coming days, I needed to center myself for the questioning I would receive. Would the Commission be fair and equitable?

But if the government restricted licensed Jewish doctors and attorneys from practicing their profession, then who was I? A man from China was lower than the Jews.

What was I to expect in a country where laws don't work the same for everyone?

On the Collingwood shoreline, I vowed to endure to the end. Caitlin encouraged me to be myself during the hearing, and I was comforted to know that she'd be next to me throughout the inquiry.

As the sun appeared above the horizon, I observed a woman walking to work who reminded me of NaiNai, our family's quiet matriarch. I flashed back to a day when she was watching me play and said, "I want to talk to you. Let's go sit by ourselves outside."

I obeyed, and when we sat next to each other on a bench, she put her arm around me and said, "I want to tell you a secret, you're going to be a special young man." Her eyes twinkled, "I want you to promise to do the right thing throughout your life."

"Yes, NaiNai, I promise."

"Even when it's the hardest thing for you to do. Promise me."

"I promise NaiNai."

I was raised to do the right thing and to be mindful of character.

I made my way back to the hotel to dress and have breakfast with Caitlin. We walked hand in hand to Parliament Hill and entered East Block, where a tall, slightly overweight security guard checked our credentials and led us up a flight of stairs to a room on the second floor.

He opened the door, and when I tried to escort Caitlin in, he put his arm out to stop her, then said, "I'm sorry, Madam, but you aren't allowed to enter."

"Sir, she's my wife."

"My orders are that the meeting will be held in private and only with you."

"We planned to be together during the hearing."

"I'm sorry, Sir. I have my orders."

"She's my wife."

Caitlin took hold of my arm, and in a low voice said, "Honey, it's okay. I'll wait in a nearby room."

"Madam, there is no waiting area. I'll have someone escort you back downstairs."

She gripped my hand, strained a smile, and her eyes flitted. I regretted leaving her alone.

"Please, let me have a minute with my wife."

He nodded and then moved a few steps away but continued to watch us as if we were convicts.

I softly said, "Take the day touring Ottawa and let's plan to meet back at the hotel late this afternoon."

When she squeezed my hand, I could tell she didn't want to leave my side, but I hoped sightseeing would provide her a diversion. When another guard approached us, the man in front of us said, "Madam, you have to go now, and this officer will escort you to an exit."

She whispered in my ear, "Arm yourself in my love. I am always with you."

I kissed her cheek and was unnerved when we released each other's hands.

I watched her until she was out of sight.

Now we were both alone.

I entered a large conference room with a high ceiling, large paned windows, and portraits on the walls. There was a long, rectangular, straight-grained dark-walnut conference table surrounded by high-backed, overstuffed leather chairs.

The notice stated the special Commission would be comprised of five members, and as the door slowly swung open, four men wearing dark suits, donning long coats and hats, entered. I read that communists all wore the same type of clothing. Was this to be a similar group?

When a tall man with gaunt features, grey hair, and dandruff on the shoulders of his charcoal suit approached me, I felt like an unsophisticated interloper.

"Mr. LeBlanc, I'm Gustave Justin." He introduced me to the other Commission members who walked in behind him, then said, "We are waiting for our last member to join us."

I was nervous and felt the hard stares from these stiff and formal men when the door slowly opened, and a tall, elegant woman wearing a business suit and carrying a fur coat entered. Mr. Justin introduced me to Miss Ellen Jerome. I stood, greeted her, and introduced myself as Winson LeBlanc, also known as Tao Wen Shun.

After she apologized for being late, Mr. Justin said, "Now let's get started."

A stenographer sat at one end of the table, and I was at the other end. The Commissioners took their chairs on the sides as a young girl entered and placed files in front of them. Then a black man in a white uniform rolled in a cart with beverages and served hot drinks. He asked if I'd like tea or coffee, I asked for water.

Then Mr. Justin requested all staff to leave the room, except for the stenographer, and when he said, "We have many questions to put before you," I told myself to pause and weigh every word before I spoke.

The morning was spent reviewing the information obtained on my background and answering questions regarding my history of leaving China, coming to Vancouver, and then Collingwood.

We took a break for lunch, but I had no appetite. I was drained and desperately needed air. It was a good walk back to the hotel, and I didn't know if Caitlin would be there, so I walked the grounds around the Capital, stopped at an overlook, and leaned against the railing. I looked down the steep cliff at the Ottawa River, which divided the provinces of Ontario and Quebec.

Then from behind me, I heard an unpleasant but familiar voice speaking Mandarin. "Tao Wen Shun, or is it Zhu Yao, or Winson LeBlanc. What should I call you?"

It was a harsh voice, one I hoped to never hear again. I turned and was face to face with Tak.

"You think you can escape from us by changing your name, clothes, or appearance?"

An unexpected coldness hit my core. I looked around to see if there was anyone else.

Everything he did was forceful as he aggressively walked toward me. I wanted to pull back from him, but I could feel the railing against my back.

"We have the power to destroy you. We can tell the government the truth about who you are, that you're illegal. We know everything about you."

"What do you know about me?" I snapped, and his hard stare told me he took my question as an impertinence.

"Your parents met our agent, Zhang, in Hangzhou. Bruno drilled you with details for your new identity. Jovi paid off the Vancouver Immigration agent. You're only a paper son who entered the country with fraudulent documentation."

He glared at me for a long moment, then gritted his teeth. "We can take everything away from you, your citizenship, your bank, your home, and your Irish wife."

He looked for a reaction. I was stunned with what he disclosed, but I'd show him nothing when confronted like this.

"We have contacts within the RCMP looking for people like you. I can make a call, and you'll be disgraced. Or you can cooperate with us, and we'll remain silent."

His stare was hard-edged, and there was nothing pleasant about him. "We can work together so you can keep your little white family. There's no Chinese girl who'd take you now that you have slept with a foreign devil, a gweipo."

He moved closer and pushed me hard into the railing. I lifted my arms to put space between us, pushing him back. What was he doing in Ottawa and on Parliament Hill? Was he called to testify before the Commission? That would explain how the Commission obtained my names and background information. Should I give in to this man to save myself, my marriage?

I needed to stall for time, to think. "Do you have a cigarette?"

His malicious smile revealed yellow-stained teeth and blackened gums. He pulled a pack of cigarettes from his pocket and leaned it toward me. I took one, then he did too. He pulled out and flicked open his lighter, lit his cigarette, and then mine. I took a step to move away from being between him and the railing.

I took a drag and wanted to feel a release of tension, but it didn't happen.

Tak said, "In Canada, you will always be a *Wai Sheng Ren*, an 'outsider.' Working with us, at least you will be with people you understand."

I lowered my eyes because he was right. I had been asked many times by strangers how I could afford such expensive clothes. Then, there were the disdainful expressions on people's faces when Caitlin and I were together in public, and they looked at me as if I was committing a crime.

He continued, "We're a community and have our networks in China and Canada. You saw how it works when you escaped and the police returned you to camp."

I looked up and his intense stare was unsettling.

"What have you heard from your family since leaving China?"

I tried not to show any reaction, but I must have because he puffed up as if he had hooked a helpless fish. He knew I hadn't received any letters or contact from my family.

A tall, thin security guard with sharp facial features, black hair, eyes, and mustache was patrolling the grounds and broke my thoughts as he walked toward us. I nervously looked at him, wanting to reach out for help, but what could he do?

The guard stopped in an all too familiar posture and looked at me intently. He was smoking a cigarette and I could tell by the smell, it was the same brand Tak smoked. Did he happen to arrive just when Tak did?

I was caught between two worlds, I didn't want to return to Dung's, and the establishment didn't want me in theirs.

Tak looked at the guard and then grinned at me as if the guard was his friend. He continued to speak in Mandarin, "We know your mother is laboring in the rice paddies. She was foolish to think a woman could be educated and teach men."

I was stunned. How could Tak have that information, and was it true? "How do you know about Mother?"

Tak was reading my every reaction. "Our network is extensive, and we have the means to bring her here."

He had the hook in me, I had taken the bait, and now he was preparing to gaff me.

"We just want your cooperation." He said softly.

Cooperation to men like Tak, meant control. What was he after? Was it the bank or my house?

If he knew about my mother, what else did they know about my family?

"Do you know where my sister is?" My voice cracked and when I raised my eyebrows he grinned as he said, "Of course."

"What about my grandfather?"

He shook his head, "He is dead."

I dropped my head even though it was what I suspected.

Thinking of the choice my parents made for me and the aftermath of what they experienced under Mao, now given an opportunity, how could I not try to do the same for them?

Tak and Dung's networks were capable of locating my family and bringing them to Canada through bribery and extortion. I could not envision any other means that could extricate my family.

But at what cost?

They would want some ownership of the bank at a minimum, but once they gained that, like cancer, they would eventually seize control. They would undoubtedly require a percentage upfront and would later alter any agreement like they did with my indenture. And there would be no assurance that they could bring my family out of China or even try to honor their word.

I didn't like gambling when I was on the ship, and this was a high stakes game forcing me to gamble with all that I owned. Either way, my family somewhere in China was at stake, but I also had my life with Caitlin to consider and my word and pledge to Julian. If Tak and Dung became involved with the bank, I would not be able to carry out Julian's directives nor protect the employees or ourselves.-

The guard yelled, "You screaming chinks need to move on. Just 'cause you're dressed in fancy suits don't mean nothin' with me. I know your type, and it doesn't belong around here."

His smear somehow snapped me back to reality. Darkness hides a world that some call an underworld, inhabited by creatures brought to life by night. Sometimes we see a glimpse into their shadowy lives, and there are times when we see who they are as clear as day. They think their ugly behavior is masked by fancy clothes and trappings, but I have seen them exposed in the light, and I could never trust Tak or Dung.

For all I wanted to do for my parents, I knew they would sacrifice their lives once again for me and would not want me to cooperate or participate in any way with evil men.

Tak hissed and cursed the guard in Mandarin and hearing his inflection triggered memories of the workcamp and how Tak had utter disdain and contempt for the law.

I looked at him and saw him stiffen and put his hand near the bulge in his coat pocket. I questioned if he would pull a gun on the guard on Parliament Hill?

Facing the guard, Tak spread his legs and planted his feet. His dark grey pinstripe suit, polished shoes, and groomed hair gave a professional appearance, but underneath he was a gangster.

While Tak and the guard faced each other, I stepped away.

Tak uttered profanities at me. "You're a *gwaijai*. You'll never be finished with us!"

I kept walking.

"It's a shame what befell Suk and his prostitute wife," Tak yelled.

I stopped and cringed, I wanted to confront him, but that's what he wanted. I kept my back to him but felt vulnerable.

"Don't you want to know about Lijuan, your little doll-faced baby sister?" he sneered.

I shuddered.

He knew my sister's name. From Mr. Wong's reports, anxiety over my family's safety increasingly had consumed me, and I wondered if this might be my only opportunity to learn what happened to Lijuan?

My muscles tensed. I desperately wanted to turn around and inquire about Lijuan. I also wanted to punch him for calling her doll-faced, liked Zhang the feeder agent did back in Hangzhou.

I closed my eyes as I put my hand over YeYe's medallion and felt it under my shirt and tie. NaiNai told me to always do what's right, no matter the cost.

I started to walk away but stopped when he said, "We know you're staying at the Chateau."

My nails dug into my palms. Did he know that Caitlin had come with me?

I took a deep breath and turned around to look at him. I wanted to read his expression, hoping to learn something about how much he knew about Caitlin.

The guard was watching and listening and had his hand on his holster as Tak continued in Mandarin, "It's sad that you're in the meeting without your wife. But then, you can't hide behind her skirt."

The blood pounded in my ears, my heart thudded, and my hands shook. I stepped toward Tak but then abruptly stopped when the guard barked, "That's enough. I ought to haul you two Charlie Chan's down to the department."

If I was arrested, I'd miss my meeting, and the security guard would never believe that I was in a Commission hearing in East Block, and I didn't have anything on me to prove it. If I missed the meeting, the Commission would assume the worst, and I'd be in jail with Tak.

"You two break up your yellow lingo and move on."

As I walked away, Tak muttered, "I would've killed you after we took your shoe money."

His statement surprised me. I had wondered if Dung had allowed me to live because of the snake. Had he looked the other way like Eng?

I didn't have time to ponder the subject, Caitlin was sightseeing somewhere in Ottawa, and I needed to find her and warn her about Tak. I'd be late for the meeting, but that wasn't my priority.

I ran to the Chateau, but she was out. I left an urgent message with the front desk and told them she needed to wait for me at the hotel and not go out again.

I rushed back for the Commission meeting, and as I walked in, Gustave Justin gave me a stern squinty-eyed look, glanced at the wall clock, and watched me take my seat. With a sharp edge, he said, "Perhaps you misunderstood the time we were to reconvene."

"I want to apologize to the Commission for my tardiness. It was unintentional due to extenuating circumstances. Please let me explain."

I sighed deeply and then told them how Tak had confronted me during the lunch break, tried to bribe me, and threatened my wife.

Justin curtly said, "That's enough."

Miss Jerome interrupted him, "You're right Justin. We should take a recess while we engage the RCMP to put out a search for Mrs. LeBlanc and this Tak person. Winson, do you have a picture of your wife? Can you provide us the full name and description of Tak?"

Justin looked annoyingly at Miss Jerome as I pulled the picture I always kept of her in my wallet and provided a physical description and where I thought she might be touring in the city. Then I gave her a physical description and both names he might use, Tao-ching and Tak, and said that he was associated with the Imperial Lumber Company in Vancouver.

Miss Jerome looked at Justin as she said, "All of us here will do what we can to provide for her safety. Please excuse me for a few minutes while I speak to the guard."

Justin said, "We're limited by our availability and need to conclude this proceeding by tomorrow. Are you able to continue when Miss Jerome returns?"

"Yes, Sir."

I had a few moments to collect myself, and when Miss Jerome returned, she made eye contact with me and said, "The RCMP has been contacted and are putting out an all-points bulletin for Caitlin and for this Tak character."

As they reopened the folders in front of them, I took a deep breath, trying to release my stress. My physical and emotional energy was spent, and all I could do was trust that Caitlin was safe.

I spent the remainder of the day detailing circumstances that occurred from the time I left Hangzhou. I told them as much as I could recall about Dung's operation.

The Commissioners took detailed notes, and just before four, Justin said, "This concludes the questions we have for you.

You are now excused. We will continue to meet in a private session to review information and will reconvene tomorrow morning promptly at eight."

I was exhausted and distressed as I left the conference room. When the door opened behind me, I heard raised voices and a heated discussion, and Miss Jerome came into the hallway and asked to speak to me away from the other members.

"I understand the discrimination you have been subjected to. I have experienced discrimination for most of my adult life. Not ethnic discrimination, but because I'm a woman. I do the same job as men, yet don't receive the same pay for equivalent work. All people should be viewed equally without regard to race or gender."

I marveled at her courage and her statement of discrimination toward women. I said, "There is a passage in *The Plague* by Camus that says the plague never dies for good, it can remain dormant for years in various places until it reawakens its carriers and sends them forth again into the world. Discrimination is like the plague bacillus, it never vanishes for good, and there are always 'rats' to spread the infection to others."

She raised her eyebrows, then smiled and pulled out her business card, "I want you to call me as soon as you know anything about your wife."

After talking to Miss Jerome, I hurried to the hotel and was greeted by William the bellman, "Welcome back to the Chateau, Mr. LeBlanc."

"Hello William, have you seen my wife?"

"Why no, Mr. LeBlanc, I haven't. But I only just came on duty a few minutes ago."

I scanned the lobby for Caitlin, then rushed to our room. Opening the door, I called her name, but there was no answer. I looked to see if there was any evidence of her and noticed a note on the pillow. All I could think of was Tak's threats and cruelty. Was this how he'd inform me of what had happened to her?

It felt like my heart stopped, and sweat erupted through every pore as I unfolded the note and read, "My love, I hope you had a good day! I got your message when I came back from lunch. I'm on the rooftop reading a book by the pool. I miss you."

I rushed up to the rooftop, and when I saw my beautiful wife, I gave her a long hug, pressed her close, and didn't want to release her, and when I did, she looked at me and asked, "Are you okay? Did something happen in the meeting?"

I relayed the events of the day, who was at the meeting, and what we discussed. I told her about going to the river overlook during lunch, the confrontation with Tak, and his remarks about my sister and Suk. I didn't reveal his veiled threat concerning her but ended by telling her about Miss Jerome's concern and willingness to help.

We decided to stay in the hotel and have dinner in the dining room. While Caitlin was getting ready for dinner, I called Miss Jerome and asked if she could obtain permission for Caitlin to join tomorrow's meeting because of Tak's threat. When she said yes, I could relax and enjoy the evening but had no appetite.

⁓

The next morning, the Commission reconvened promptly at 8:00 am. Mr. Andrews, a man with dark eyes, small low-set ears, and receding grey hair, who hardly said a word in yesterday's meeting, sat in Mr. Justin's chair at the head of the table and tapped his spoon against his teacup. When he had everyone's attention, he cleared his throat and said, "Mr. Justin has recused himself from this morning's proceedings and asked me to carry on in his place. I am now calling the meeting to order."

I thought it peculiar that Justin was not present, but then Andrews looked at Caitlin and said, "Mrs. LeBlanc, we have made an exception and are glad you have joined us today."

He glanced at a paper and then addressed me, "Mr. LeBlanc, we have reviewed your history and circumstances of entry into Canada. We understand that your parents did what they thought was in your best interest. They were unaware of the ethics of the organization that provided you the opportunity to come to Canada.

"Your citizenship is not in question. We wanted to hear your story of how you got into Canada. We have many concerns regarding illegal immigration in our country and have formed a new committee to address Chinese and Asian immigration issues."

He stopped and closed the folder in front of him, then pushed his chair back. "Mr. LeBlanc, by a majority vote, we'd like you to consider an appointment to this new committee. Miss Jerome, will you please provide further comment."

"Thank you, Mr. Andrews. In 1959, the Department of Immigration discovered a problem with immigration papers used by Chinese immigrants to enter Canada. The Royal Canadian Mounted Police were brought in to investigate. It turned out Chinese had been entering Canada by purchasing real or fake birth certificates of Chinese Canadian children bought and sold in Hong Kong and mainland China. These children carrying false identity papers, like yourself, were referred to as 'Paper Sons.'

Winson, we believe you're one of these paper sons. In response, we, as a Commission, are recommending to Parliament a program called the 'Chinese Adjustment Statement Program.' This program will grant amnesty for paper sons or daughters if they come forward and confess their conditions of entry into Canada to the government. Our hope is that this program will lead to fair and equitable immigration of Chinese into Canada by eliminating the *Race and Place of Origin* sections of our immigration policy. Chinese Canadians will finally feel they're no longer institutionally discriminated against in Canadian society."

I was relieved as I looked over at Caitlin. The smile on her face and the sparkle in her eyes allowed me to finally relax. Caitlin and I spent several hours that afternoon with Miss Jerome, going over how she envisioned my role on the committee. My hope was that I could help other Chinese who had also immigrated under false pretenses.

∽

Early the next morning, we checked out and went to the train station to catch the first train for Collingwood. After purchasing two seats at the ticket window, we stopped at the Brasserie Coffee Shop to buy tea and chocolate croissants to have on the train. I scanned the surrounding area for Tak or anyone of Chinese descent.

We were in line behind an older lady carrying an overnight bag, and behind us were two Anglo businessmen dressed in dark suits, each with a newspaper under his arm. One was stocky with short legs and a long torso, and the other was tall and thin.

Caitlin and I strolled hand in hand to the platform designated for that morning's train to Collingwood. I was looking forward to putting the events of the past few days and weeks behind us and returning to the comfort of home. We were standing about ten feet from the edge of the platform when I checked the clock on the pole and saw that the train was due in five minutes.

I was looking down the tracks in the direction the train was to arrive when I heard, "Hi doll, you're a sweet little bird."

Tak was standing behind Caitlin with his left hand gripping her left arm and his right hand in his coat pocket, poking something into her back. There was terror in her eyes as she dropped her tea.

I stepped between her and the tracks as he pushed her toward the edge of the platform. In Mandarin, Tak said, "Nice to find you and your gweipo together," then in English, "If either of you screams, I will push her off the platform and onto the tracks."

"You keep her out of this. It's me you want to deal with. Let her go, and I'll speak to you." I answered in Mandarin.

"You know what we have discussed."

"The $1,000?"

Caitlin's lips were quivering, and I could see her body shaking. As I inched closer to her, he jerked her away from me, and she whimpered.

"We have helped you be in a position to own a bank. Don't you think we're entitled to participate in the fruits of your good fortune?"

There must be a gun in his pocket because Caitlin winced as he shoved whatever he was holding harder into her back and pushed her toward the edge of the platform. I saw fear in her eyes. I took hold of her right arm, and Tak still had her left.

The public address system announced the arrival of our train, which was rumbling into the station.

"You aren't foolish enough to shoot that gun on this platform. There're too many witnesses."

"No, but she can accidentally fall on the tracks while the train is arriving. You'll determine her future here and now. Do you want to lose your wife to an avoidable accident over a bit of money? Everyone can have what they want, but the choice is yours."

I'd give my life, the bank, our house, everything I had, as long as Caitlin was safe. But I didn't think Tak and Dung would ever be satisfied. Their greed and power consumed them.

There were blows of the train's air horn as brakes shrieked from steel wheels on steel rails. Tak looked ruthless as he tightened his grip on my wife. When I saw the two businessmen move toward us, I thought about screaming at them for help but knew Tak would push Caitlin off the platform. "Let her go, I'll give you whatever you want."

"Your house is too big for two people and…"

Suddenly, the stocky businessman pulled Tak's arms backward, and the taller man grabbed Tak's wrist, then pulled Caitlin out of harm's way. "Let go of the lady and take your hand out of your pocket very slowly."

Tak turned his head and pulled a pistol out of his pocket. Then the husky man said, "I'm Detective Sergeant Bennet, and this is Detective Morgan. We're with the Ottawa Police Department and are placing you under arrest on probable grounds of intent to commit extortion and bodily harm, and possession of a firearm. You have the right to remain silent and the right to retain and instruct counsel without delay."

Detective Morgan pried the gun from Tak's hand and placed handcuffs on his wrists with his arms behind his back.

Tak hissed at me in Mandarin, "You'll never be finished with us. You don't know Dung, I won't be in jail for long."

Detective Sargent Bennet said to me, "We'd like a statement from you, but if you need to take this train, we can follow up with you by phone. Miss Jerome asked us to watch after you and your wife and make sure you were safely on the train."

"Thank you, Detective. We owe both of you our lives. I think you will understand that we'd like to get on the train and don't want to stay any longer than necessary in Ottawa," I replied.

Caitlin clung to my arm and was trembling as she said, "Thank you both, and please thank Miss Jerome for coming to our rescue."

They were pulling Tak away as the train came to a stop alongside the platform.

After we boarded, Caitlin asked what Tak said in Mandarin. I relayed the conversation and told her that Miss Jerome said they'd be investigating Dung's operation. We were exhausted and glad to leave Ottawa with the assurance that I was a Canadian citizen, and we had uncontested ownership of the bank and our home but were totally drained by the events of the last two days.

Taking our seats, Caitlin took my hand and asked, "Would you say a prayer for us?"

She had never asked me to pray, and her request alarmed me. She was pregnant and had experienced trauma from all that we encountered in Ottawa. "Are you okay? I mean, are both of you alright?"

"I know what you mean. I think we are both fine."

"I know you pray regularly, but this will be my first time."

She smiled and said, "I hope this will not be your last time, my love."

I took her hand, closed my eyes, and paused, not knowing how to start. "God, I've never spoken to you. Please grant health to my wife and our little one. Thank you for saving us from Tak and help us to live in peace."

Caitlin said, "Amen," then kissed my cheek and laid her head on my shoulder.

The train whistle blew twice, and we started to glide out of the station. About a hundred yards down the track, a conductor appeared wearing a black coat and white shirt with a name tag across the breast pocket that read, Alvin.

With a broad smile, he said, "Good morning, and welcome aboard."

I swallowed hard as I handed him the tickets and said, "Good morning, Alvin."

"I hope you had a pleasant stay in Ottawa. It's a beautiful morning."

Caitlin squeezed my hand hard and lifted her head. I replied, "The day looks to be improving for us now that we are on this train." I thought it best to change subjects, "This station is magnificent."

"Everyone says the same thing the first time. We are here to provide a comfortable trip."

"We look forward to such a trip."

"If you need anything at all, please just say 'Hey George' and one of the porters will help you."

"Thank you, Alvin."

As he left, Caitlin again leaned her head on my shoulder and closed her eyes. Her body twitched several times, after which she adjusted her position. By the time we were out of the city and into the countryside, she was asleep, and I could felt her body relax.

As the train rocked along, I enjoyed the haunting beauty of the Algonquin terrain and noticed the stacked rock formations that looked like stone men pointing with an extended arm. Mr. Lawrence told me to watch for them and called them "inukshuks." He said the stones were stacked by Inuit at prominent locations to serve as markers for those looking for the right direction and safe passage. I took it as a foreshadowing of good to come because Tak was in prison, my wife was safely beside me, and we had a child on the way.

But as thoughts of Julian filled my mind, I realized the veil of protection that I had enjoyed under his presence was over, and I had to remain vigilant regarding the ongoing threats from Dung, the Irish, and I couldn't forget about Taylor.

Thinking of Mother, Father, and Lijuan and their circumstances in China made me realize how fortunate I was as Caitlin's hand slipped into mine. I turned and saw the love that filled her eyes and smiled as I looked forward to our new adventure in parenthood.

∽

On our return to Collingwood, Caitlin went with me to the Lawrence house to meet with Kai and Wei Lei. Sitting by ourselves in the kitchen, Wei Lei wasn't able to sit still and continuously played with her hair while Kai was biting his nails. When we told them what we encountered with Tak and his arrest, Wei Lei broke down and cried.

Kai said, "We are relocating to get as far away as possible from their reach."

"But Tak's under arrest, and the RCMP will be investigating Dung," I said.

Wei Lei said, "We feel vulnerable and heard that Tak had been asking questions around town about my family. My parents are in fear and feel the tiger is at the door."

"Please stay in Collingwood. We'll help you," Caitlin pleaded.

"How can you protect us from Dung?" Kai asked me.

"The government is going to provide amnesty and citizenship for all of us. Both of you and Wei Lei's family will be legal citizens. I'll be on the Immigration Committee and do all I can to make sure it happens."

"How will this so-called amnesty safeguard us from Dung?" Wei Lei asked. Her facial expression revealed a deeper concern, protecting her from others, like the Metzger's.

I didn't have an answer, and my heart felt like it had a hole in it.

Kai said, "They have the RCMP in their pockets. It's just a matter of time before they come for us. It is too easy for them to find us in Collingwood."

Wei Lei and Caitlin cried, and Kai couldn't sit any longer, as he smoked while he paced back and forth.

"Please think about it before you make a final decision," I said.

The next evening, we met again with Kai and Wei Lei. She solemnly said, "Our family is moving north to the mining town of Timmins. My father's cousin found jobs for us at a Chinese restaurant, and Kai will work in the mines."

I said to Kai, "I don't want you to work in the mines like my YeYe's father."

"It's too late. With all of us working, we plan to save enough money to return to China." Kai said as he took a deep breath, and his eyes were glassy.

"That's a mistake. It'll be worse there under Mao," I replied as I thought about Mr. Wong's reports on conditions in China and my father's situation. I still had not told Kai I wanted to find his family.

Kai's face tightened as he said, "Remember when Jackson gave us pop?"

I smiled, "How could I forget."

"The next time we had it, he told us to shake the bottle and then open it. We shook it and, when we removed the cap, the carbonation exploded and soda spilled all over us."

I started laughing.

With sternness in his eyes, he continued, "This country has shaken me too much, and either I will return home or explode." Kai adamantly shook his head and added, "We've been through a lot together. I wouldn't be here or married if it weren't for you."

He hugged me and whispered in my ear, "This isn't the life we were cut out for. We'll never be accepted in this white man's society."

As we embraced and said goodbye, I said, "We have been together through so much from the time we left Hangzhou. I will miss you, brother, and I hope you return to Collingwood someday. We'll come for you in Timmons when I have a better alternative for you."

A few days later, when they left town in the middle of the night, a part of me died. That night I had a dream and saw Kai on the Hangzhou dock with my parents.

Catherine and Mr. Lawrence missed Wei Lei. Rhoda worked part-time with Catherine and cooked meals until we could find another helper.

∞

In the following month, I was officially appointed to a select Committee serving the Immigration Commission. The Committee was appointed to address illegal immigration and to recommend a program of reformation.

What I came to learn was the *Chinese Adjustment Statement Program* was announced after I departed from Hangzhou. The program included measures to curtail the illegal entry of Chinese into Canada. This initiative followed the crackdown of a large-scale unlawful immigration scheme, involving 'paper families' of which I had been a part. The group which ran the work camp headed by Dung was part of an extensive snakehead network, including Zhang, the feeder agent, who arranged for boys from Hangzhou and other provinces to immigrate to Canada. The Canadian government and the RCMP were investigating the operations of Imperial Lumber, Dung, and Tak.

∞

Three months later, I was asked to give an opening statement at the Immigration Commission's first public hearing before Parliament in Ottawa. As Caitlin and I walked the steps to Centre Block, locked arm in arm, I stopped abruptly when a blustery wind kicked up.

"What is wrong?" Caitlin asked.

I closed my eyes and sighed deeply.

"Winson, are you okay?"

I looked at my lovely wife and said, "I remember the day I stepped onto the ship from the dock in Hangzhou, and a stout wind was in my face. I paused then, not knowing what I'd face in the future. This feels eerily the same."

"The difference is you have me with you, and our baby is on the way."

I squeezed her hand.

She added, "And what you learned from Julian and Catherine that changed your life. The condition of your birth should not determine the outcome of your life."

Author's Note

*U*npunished Crimes is the third novel in the Collingwood Series and will be available in late 2021. To follow Winson and Caitlin's story, please see the excerpt from Chapter One that follows.

UNPUNISHED CRIMES

third novel of the the Collingwood Series

George Fillis

Chapter One

Collingwood, Ontario | 1967

"Keep your face to the sunshine,
and you can never see the shadow." –Helen Keller

On a Sunday night just after midnight, Caitlin woke with a scream. Turning on the lamp and seeing the sheets stained with blood, I panicked. "What happened? You're bleeding! Are you in pain?"

"I don't know what happened, I felt wet, and it startled me. I need to go to the hospital." With that, she started crying uncontrollably.

As I bundled her in warm clothes, she shouted, "What's happening to me? Please, God, don't let me lose the baby."

In a driving snowstorm, the streets were quiet as we rushed to the hospital. I helped Caitlin into the emergency room reception area, and we sat together in front of the admitting desk while a middle-aged attendant asked Caitlin, "What's the reason you're here?"

Caitlin told her about the bleeding.

The attendant looked at me over her glasses and said, "Sir, only family can be here. You need to take a seat over there." She pointed at several empty rows of chairs behind us.

"She's pregnant and bleeding. Something's wrong. She needs to see a doctor right away!"

"Sir, take a seat where I told you."

When I banged my fist on the desk, the attendant pushed back in her chair, her cheeks turned red as she said, "Settle down, don't raise your voice to me, or I will call security."

She glared at me and added, "You have driven her here, so now you can go back to your taxi or take a seat and wait for her. It's your choice, eh!"

"He is my husband, and I want him here," Caitlin said weakly as she put her hand on my arm.

I wanted to speak but didn't want to further upset Caitlin.

The attendant tipped her head down and looked at me over the top of her glasses. "Oh, I see," she said as she raised her pen to her mouth and stared at me, then she looked at Caitlin and continued in a measured tone, "Before you can see the doctor, we need to complete the admissions process."

"Please call Dr. Franklin, my obstetrician," Caitlin said.

"The on-duty doctor will see you first, and he will call Dr. Franklin if he is needed."

After completing the paperwork, she said, "Someone will be with you shortly. Please take a seat in the waiting area."

I helped her to a chair, then kissed her knuckles, wet from tears, and she put her head on my shoulder.

When a nurse came with a wheelchair, I helped Caitlin up, and the nurse said, "Thank you. I have her now."

"May I go in with her to see the doctor?"

"That is not allowed."

Caitlin said, "This is my husband. I want him to be with me."

She cleared her throat, looked at Caitlin, and said, "After the doctor has examined you, he will consult with your husband on your condition."

When I looked at Caitlin and saw a pained expression on her face, I felt frustrated that I couldn't be with her and helpless because it was in this same hospital that I waited on doctors treating Julian and Catherine for heart attacks.

After I let go of her hand, Caitlin and the nurse disappeared behind swinging doors with signs that read, 'Medical Staff Only.'

I paced the floor and watched the clock on the wall. After several minutes, the admissions lady stopped her paperwork and watched me with an irritated expression. As much as I tried to control my emotions, my blood was boiling. I took a step toward her, stopped, stared back, and if she wanted a further confrontation, I was prepared to give it to her.

She blinked her eyes, and when I didn't back off, she pushed her glasses up on the bridge of her nose, lowered her head, and went back to her paperwork.

Waiting alone, I sat and stared at the cold white walls, watched her fill out papers, and tried to stop my feet from bouncing up and down. I needed courage, but it was difficult to find at three in the morning.

Caitlin was in her sixth month of pregnancy, and her excitement about the baby was contagious. When we nestled together in bed, I read aloud for a while, then Caitlin would sing to the baby. Last week, she told me she could feel our little one move, so when I put my hand on her tummy and felt the movement, Caitlin remarked, "You have a big grin on your face."

Becoming a father was becoming more real for me.

Virginia had stayed with us for months but recently returned to Nova Scotia, though I wished she was with us now.

We had interesting conversations over names. Caitlin suggested naming a girl after my mother or a boy after my grandfather, although I loved Mother and YeYe, I didn't want our child to have a Chinese name, so I asked her to consider Catherine, our dearest friend, or Julian, my adoptive father. When I told her that I would defer the baby's name to her, she glowed but told me it would be a mutual decision.

The thought that it was too early in Caitlin's pregnancy for the baby to be born kept repeating in my mind. Unable to sit still, I got up and started pacing again. I looked for a payphone and wanted to call Catherine but didn't want to wake her in the middle of the night with her heart condition, so I decided to call Caitlin's parents.

Time moved slowly, but my thoughts were traveling at light speed. I needed to slow myself down, so I picked up one tattered magazine after another, thumbed through each without finding interest in any of the articles until I heard, "Winson."

Before I turned around, I recognized the deep raspy voice of Caitlin's father, Kierian Mulroney. He sounded like he was still barking commands at the shipyard, while Maureen's soft, high-pitched voice sounded like Caitlin. "Thank you for calling us. How is she?"

"I haven't heard since the nurse took her into the examination room over an hour ago. I'm waiting for the doctor."

Maureen put her hand on my arm and squeezed.

"They took her back just before I called you. They won't let me be with her."

"What happened?" Maureen asked.

As I was recounting what happened, the doors swung open, and a tall, light-skinned man wearing a green smock approached us, glanced at me, looked at Kierian, ran his fingers through his already disheveled hair, then addressed Maureen. "I am Doctor Tremblay. Are you Caitlin LeBlanc's family?"

"Yes, we are," Maureen replied as she looked at me.

"Caitlin and the baby are fine and resting comfortably. Her bleeding is from hemorrhoids, which are common during pregnancy. We gave her a local anesthetic, and the bleeding has stopped, but she experienced some mild contractions, so we would like to keep her in the hospital a few days for observation. Dr. Franklin should be in to see her before his office hours this morning."

Maureen thanked him, and when I started to ask if I could see her, the doctor turned and walked away without looking at me. I knew he heard me because Maureen gave me an embarrassed look. Although I had come to expect this behavior, it stung under the circumstances.

Kierian said, "We all should get some rest. It's been a long day."

"I want to see her before I leave. Let's check with the admissions clerk." When the clerk looked up and saw the three of us standing in front of her, I asked about Caitlin's status. She thumbed through some papers and said, "Your wife is in the process of being moved to a hospital room, and it will be hours before she will be allowed visitors."

As we stepped away, Maureen said, "Why don't you go home and try to get some rest, eh."

I knew I wouldn't be able to sleep, so I said, "I don't' want to leave her, but I will go clean up at home and return to the hospital before seven."

"Then I'll come back at nine and stay with her through the afternoon."

∽

Two days later, Caitlin returned home and was lethargic, which was understandable with all she had been through.

The following night at dinner, Caitlin said, "Kathleen is going to her family's cottage on a small private island in Georgian Bay next week. Most every summer growing up, I'd go with her for a few weeks. Her husband, Patrick, has been traveling for his work, so she invited us to join her on Pine Isle to rest and relax."

We had a sudden and puzzling loss of customers at the bank, deposit withdrawals, and staff departures. In addition, I shared oversite responsibilities for Julian's Trust with Clive Owen, which took more time than I wanted away from Caitlin. I couldn't see how I could leave and be completely out of touch on an island.

"Sweetheart, right now, I have so many issues at the bank, and as long as Dr. Franklin approves, you should go. The rest will be good for you."

"Are you certain you can't go with me?"

"We'll have the rest of our lives together. It'll be good for you to spend time with Kathleen."

"I want Kathleen to tell you about the island and hope you will change your mind and come for a few days."

∽

On Friday, when I came home from the bank, Caitlin and Kathleen were in the breakfast room having tea and Rhoda's scones. I greeted Kathleen, kissed my wife, and sat next to her.

Kathleen said, "May I pour you tea?"

"Please."

Caitlin said, "We were talking about Kathleen's family cottage on Pine Isle."

As Kathleen added milk to the tea, she said, "Winson, you both need time away. Come and stay with me."

Caitlin took my hand in hers, when our eyes met, she asked, "Sweetheart, please come with us for a few days?"

"I have too many appointments scheduled at the bank, and we are shorthanded."

"But it's so remote, and you won't be bothered by anyone. Please, do it for yourself, do it for us? Come for a week, the bank will still be here when you return."

I wanted to please Caitlin and sighed as I said, "I wish I could, but there is no stand-in for me."

Caitlin dropped her head, then looked at Kathleen and said, "Tell him about the cottage."

"My grandfather and his brothers built it out of pine logs felled from the island. A long front porch overlooks a sandy beach and sheltered bay. Inside is a dry-stack stone fireplace that goes from floor to ceiling, and the house is surrounded by a forest of birch, maple, and pine trees. There are hiking trails and pinkish-gray granite outcroppings all over the island."

"Winson, you love nature." Caitlin's voice was soft and kind, with the inflection she used to get her way with me. "We can take walks, and you won't hear any phones or customers complaining. Pine Isle is amazing and is part of an archipelago of over ten thousand islands."

I closed my eyes and reconsidered going. Caitlin was right, the rest would be good for both of us, but I couldn't neglect the bank. "Mr. Stromberger asked to see me on Wednesday, and I am meeting with Mr. Drott on Friday afternoon. I need to get out in the community and figure out why we are losing customers."

When I saw Caitlin's chin dip and her lips press tightly, I added, "I would like to go for a few weeks, but the best I can promise is to come up Friday afternoon for the last weekend."

The corners of her mouth turned up as Kathleen said, "If your circumstances change, you can always come early. We don't have phone service on our island, but if you want to come, contact my parents, and they will get word to me through Mr. Gerow, who lives on an island not far from ours. When he boats to Penetanguishene for supplies at the general store, he calls my parents when I have a message for them, and if they have a message for me, they leave it with the store. So you can always leave a message for us by calling my mother. I'll leave you her phone number."

∽

Three days later, on a Saturday morning, we drove two hours to Kathleen's boat, docked at Penetanguishene. When we pulled into the marina, I loaded their luggage and supplies, hugged and kissed Caitlin, then stood on the dock and watched as Kathleen drove the boat out into the bay. I watched the boat get smaller until it was entirely out of sight and was reminded of my family on the dock watching my ship leave Hangzhou.

On the drive back to Collingwood, massive thunderous clouds spread along the ridge of the Blue Mountains, and as the wind picked up, the clouds took the shape of a dragon before engulfing the mountains. I was overtired and thought I saw forms in the sky where there were none.

∾

Without phone service, I did not expect to hear from Caitlin during the first week. Kathleen said Gerow made trips ashore every few days for supplies and would pick-up whatever they needed and phone her parents if she had a message for them. I was looking forward to meeting the girls for the last weekend. I did not hear from Kathleen's parents and was lonely lacking daily contact with Caitlin.

On Wednesday evening of the second week, there was a loud knock at the door. When I answered, I was surprised to see Kathleen's parents, the Grahams, and invited them into the parlor.

Mr. Graham, a stout middle-aged man, looked around and, with a sharp edge, said, "This is a fancy place, eh. LeBlanc made a lot of money, charging high interest for his loans."

I bit my tongue and turned toward Mrs. Graham, a slender woman with a strong face, and asked, "Would you like something to drink?"

"We won't be here that long," he said tersely.

Mr. Graham avoided eye contact with me as he sat on the sofa. He reeked of cigarettes, and when he took a pack of Player's out of his shirt pocket, I cleared my throat and said, "I'm sorry, but we don't smoke in the house."

He glared at me, then pulled a cigarette out of the package and said, "Do you have an ashtray?"

I stared back. He was treating me like a lower-class person in my own house. I felt my temper rising, and Mrs. Graham must have sensed the tension as she said, "Frank, they don't smoke in the house. Remember, Caitlin is pregnant, and they're trying to protect the baby."

He grunted and said, "But she is not…" he stopped and scowled at me before putting the cigarette back in the pack.

Mrs. Graham was sitting on the edge of the sofa with clasped hands in her lap as she said, "We're here about the girls."

When we made eye contact, she gave me a slight smile. "Our agreement has been that Kathleen would send word back to us by way of Cornelius Gerow, a neighbor on the island next to ours. Last Sunday, we heard that all was okay. Late this afternoon, Cornelius called to say he motored to Pine Isle on Tuesday to check on the girls, but the boat and girls were gone. He went back this morning, and everything still looked the same."

"Could they have gone to another island?"

Mr. Graham snapped, "Dumbass. Cornelius said they were gone, as in missing!"

I collapsed into the chair and could feel the blood drain from my face. "My God!" I felt confused and had to clear my head. "Please give me a moment."

Mr. Graham curtly said, "I had concerns over Kathleen traveling with your wife."

"What do you mean?"

"You know." He squinted his eyes as he looked around the room.

"No, I don't. Please explain it to me."

"People around here don't like one of ours marrying your kind."

Mrs. Graham interrupted. "Frank! No! That's not what he meant, Mr. LeBlanc. He's upset."

"You're wrong." His voice intensified, "That's precisely what I meant! It's because she's married to him."

His glare had a cold emptiness, and his face reddened.

"If anything happens to Kathleen, I will hold you responsible!" He bolted up and stepped toward me.

When I stood to face him, I clenched my fists, and Mrs. Graham rose, took a firm grasp of his arm, pulled him into her, and in a calming tone said, "Now, Frank. We're here to tell Winson what we know. The girls' safety is what's important. Nothing else."

I took a step back from him, looked at her, and asked, "What can I do?"

He barked, "I told you it was a waste of time to come here. This…this idiot can't possibly be any help at all." He huffed, stomped his foot, took his wife's arm, and said, "You have already done enough! Let's go."

"Wait! Have you contacted the police?" I asked.

Mrs. Graham stopped in the doorway, lowered her head, looked at me with tears welling in her eyes, and said, "We're driving to Penetanguishene to report them missing to the Ontario Provincial Police. We'll let you know if we hear anything. Cornelius will pick us up and take us to the island."

"Let me come with you."

"Hell no!" Graham said.

Acknowledgments

A special thank you to Dr. Lew Spurlock, whose literary guidance and mentorship significantly contributed to writing this book series and my development as an author. Lew pushed me to unlock what lies within me, and that is one of the greatest gifts one can give to another.

And to my wife, Karen, for her willingness to review and edit the story, and for her encouragement, love and presence in my life.

I also want to thank my many gifted proofreading and editing partners who have graciously given me constructive criticism and sound advice.

Many thanks to Doug Burlock for his permission to use one of his wonderful photos, Winter Shoreline, for the book cover. Doug took this sunrise photo of the Inukshuk at Sunset Point Park in Collingwood with Georgian Bay frozen in the foreground.

About the Author

George Fillis, the son of Greek immigrants, is the author of the Collingwood Series. A graduate of Trinity University, he lives in San Antonio, Texas, with his wife, Karen. He discovered his passion for writing after careers in securities, real estate, and biotech. Inspired by travels to China and Canada, he heard a remarkable story about a 'paper son,' which was the seed for *A Heart To Survive* and *An Unexpected Father*.

Hearing individual stories about immigrants awakens something in him, especially those filled with hope for a better life and the courage to overcome overwhelming odds. Although this is a story of coming to Canada, it could be anywhere.

He hopes this book series generates awareness about courage, what it means to stand alone in the face of overwhelming odds, the importance of character, always choosing to do what is right, and understanding what it is like to live outside of one's comfort zone. All of these come at a cost."

Discussion Questions

1. Do you believe that even in the worst circumstances, if you believe in yourself, you will find the heart to survive?

2. Have you ever met someone not of your flesh and blood, but of your heart?

3. Do you make decisions based on what's in the best interest of others?

4. Have you experienced circumstances that have pushed you beyond your comfort zone?

5. If you believe we all are equal in death, then should we be equal in life?

6. Do you enjoy books written in first person?

7. Were the characters believable?

8. What was your favorite part of the book?

9. What was your least favorite?

10. Which scene has stuck with you the most?

11. Do you agree with this statement, "Always do what's right, no matter the cost?"

12. How has your parent's or grandparents' legacy impacted your life?

13. Do you believe the condition of your birth affects the outcome of your life?

A Discussion with George Fillis

Q. Do you find writing therapeutic?

A. I learn more about myself through the process of writing stories, discovering a creativity and a release of expression within me that continually amazes me in the true sense of the word. When crafting a storyline based on people experiencing real events and then dramatizing plots around these data points, I become fully connected to the characters.

Q. Tell us a little about how this story first came to be. Did it start with an image, a voice, a concept, a dilemma, or something else?

A. Hearing individual stories about immigrants awakens something in me because of the parallel to my family's coming to America. Especially those filled with hope for a better life and the courage to overcome overwhelming odds.

Several years ago, when my wife and I traveled to Collingwood, Ontario, and one night when we were at dinner, I met an Irish Canadian woman who shared her remarkable life story of marrying a Chinese 'paper son.' She told us of his immigration and life as a human chattel. I was looking for a unique story and started researching Paper Families.

I read tales of hardships, resilience, and passion that not only explored the depth of human desires but drove home the bitter realities of racism in 1950s Canada. It took me on a journey into the historical past of two nations divided by culture and continents.

Q. Tell us some more about your book.

A. It is a 20th-century historical fiction novel about the plight of human trafficking victims and how one of those victims, Tao Wen Shun or Winson, went through a heart-wrenching experience of separation from his family and entrance into a tumultuous new world. The story begins in China in 1949 during a bloody civil war and continues to a Canadian society where Winson is judged based on his skin color and racial background.

Although this is a story of coming to Canada, it could be anywhere. The hardships of immigration are brought to life through Winson's struggles, and his triumphs are aided by the intervention of people he encounters in his journey.

Q. What do you hope readers will take away from this story?

A. First, to learn about courage and what it means to stand alone in the face of overwhelming odds; second, the importance of character and always choosing to do what is right; and third, understanding what it is like to live outside of one's comfort zone. All of these come at a cost.

Q. How do you come up with names for your characters?

A. I keep a journal of intriguing names and their meanings when meeting people from various ethnic backgrounds. In writing this story, I auditioned names with characters, and from living with them, the name and personality eventually find each other. I changed the names of many characters, but Winson's remained constant.

Q. What's more important: characters or plot?

A. Both elements are at work. Initially, this story is plot-driven, as the protagonist faces events beyond his control. But in the end, I think it is the characters that move the story forward and either charm or anger the reader.

Q. Which character was most challenging to create? Why?

A. A villain in the story is a man named Dung. It was straightforward to give him evil characteristics. Still, we are all multifaceted and not all good or bad, so to provide good qualities and create a back story to illicit compassion for who he had become made him the most challenging character to develop.

Made in the USA
Columbia, SC
23 July 2021